WHEN YOU REACH ME

Rebecca Stead

WENDY
LAMB
BOOKS

Published by Wendy Lamb Books
an imprint of Random House Children's Books
a division of Random House, Inc.
New York

Visit us on the Web! www.randomhouse.com/kids

Educators and librarians, for a variety of teaching tools, visit us at
www.randomhouse.com/teachers

Library of Congress Cataloging-in-Publication Data
Stead, Rebecca.
When you reach me / Rebecca Stead. — 1st ed.
p. cm.
Summary: As her mother prepares to be a contestant on the 1970s television game show, "The $20,000 Pyramid," a twelve-year-old New York City girl tries to make sense of a series of mysterious notes received from an anonymous source that seems to defy the laws of time and space.
ISBN 978-0-385-73742-5 (hardcover) — ISBN 978-0-385-90664-7 (Gibraltar lib. bdg.)
ISBN 978-0-375-89269-1 (e-book) [1. Space and time—Fiction. 2. New York (N.Y.)—History—Fiction.] I. Title.
PZ7.S80857Wh 2009
[Fic]—dc22
2008024998

The text of this book is set in 12-point Village.

Book design by Kate Gartner

Printed in the United States of America

20 19 18 17

First Edition

To Sean, Jack, and Eli,
champions of inappropriate laughter, fierce love,
and extremely deep questions

The most beautiful experience
we can have
is the mysterious.

—Albert Einstein
The World As I See It (1931)

Things You Keep in a Box

So Mom got the postcard today. It says *Congratulations* in big curly letters, and at the very top is the address of Studio TV-15 on West 58th Street. After three years of trying, she has actually made it. She's going to be a contestant on *The $20,000 Pyramid*, which is hosted by Dick Clark.

On the postcard there's a list of things to bring. She needs some extra clothes in case she wins and makes it to another show, where they pretend it's the next day even though they really tape five in one afternoon. Barrettes are optional, but she should definitely bring some with her. Unlike me, Mom has glossy red hair that bounces around and might obstruct America's view of her small freckled face.

And then there's the date she's supposed to show up, scrawled in blue pen on a line at the bottom of the card: *April 27, 1979.* Just like you said.

I check the box under my bed, which is where I've kept your notes these past few months. There it is, in your tiny handwriting: *April 27th: Studio TV-15, the*

1

words all jerky-looking, like you wrote them on the subway. Your last "proof."

I still think about the letter you asked me to write. It nags at me, even though you're gone and there's no one to give it to anymore. Sometimes I work on it in my head, trying to map out the story you asked me to tell, about everything that happened this past fall and winter. It's all still there, like a movie I can watch when I want to. Which is never.

Things That Go Missing

Mom has swiped a big paper calendar from work and Scotch-taped the month of April to the kitchen wall. She used a fat green marker, also swiped from work, to draw a pyramid on April 27, with dollar signs and exclamation points all around it. She went out and bought a fancy egg timer that can accurately measure a half minute. They don't have fancy egg timers in the supply closet at her office.

April twenty-seventh is also Richard's birthday. Mom wonders if that's a good omen. Richard is Mom's boyfriend. He and I are going to help Mom practice every single night, which is why I'm sitting at my desk instead of watching after-school TV, which is a birthright of every latchkey child. "Latchkey child" is a name for a kid with keys who hangs out alone after school until a grown-up gets home to make dinner. Mom hates that expression. She says it reminds her of dungeons, and must have been invented by someone strict and awful with an unlimited child-care budget. "Probably someone German," she says, glaring at Richard, who is German but not strict or awful.

It's possible. In Germany, Richard says, I would be one of the *Schlüsselkinder*, which means "key children."

"You're lucky," he tells me. "Keys are power. Some of us have to come knocking." It's true that he doesn't have a key. Well, he has a key to *his* apartment, but not to ours.

Richard looks the way I picture guys on sailboats—tall, blond, and very tucked-in, even on weekends. Or maybe I picture guys on sailboats that way because Richard loves to sail. His legs are very long, and they don't really fit under our kitchen table, so he has to sit kind of sideways, with his knees pointing out toward the hall. He looks especially big next to Mom, who's short and so tiny she has to buy her belts in the kids' department and make an extra hole in her watchband so it won't fall off her arm.

Mom calls Richard Mr. Perfect because of how he looks and how he knows everything. And every time she calls him Mr. Perfect, Richard taps his right knee. He does that because his right leg is shorter than his left one. All his right-foot shoes have two-inch plat-forms nailed to the bottom so that his legs match. In bare feet, he limps a little.

"You should be grateful for that leg," Mom tells him. "It's the only reason we let you come around." Richard has been "coming around" for almost two years now.

*   *   *

We have exactly twenty-one days to get Mom ready for the game show. So instead of watching television, I'm copying words for her practice session tonight. I write each word on one of the white index cards Mom swiped from work. When I have seven words, I bind the cards together with a rubber band she also swiped from work.

I hear Mom's key in the door and flip over my word piles so she can't peek.

"Miranda?" She clomps down the hall—she's on a clog kick lately—and sticks her head in my room. "Are you starving? I thought we'd hold dinner for Richard."

"I can wait." The truth is I've just eaten an entire bag of Cheez Doodles. After-school junk food is another fundamental right of the latchkey child. I'm sure this is true in Germany, too.

"You're sure you're not hungry? Want me to cut up an apple for you?"

"What's a kind of German junk food?" I ask her. "Wiener crispies?"

She stares at me. "I have no idea. Why do you ask?"

"No reason."

"Do you want the apple or not?"

"No, and get out of here—I'm doing the words for later."

"Great." She smiles and reaches into her coat pocket. "Catch." She lobs something toward me, and I grab what turns out to be a bundle of brand-new markers in rainbow colors, held together with a fat rubber band. She clomps back toward the kitchen.

Richard and I figured out a while ago that the more stuff Mom swipes from the office supply closet, the more she's hating work. I look at the markers for a second and then get back to my word piles.

Mom has to win this money.

Things You Hide

I was named after a criminal. Mom says that's a dramatic way of looking at things, but sometimes the truth is dramatic.

"The name Miranda stands for people's rights," she said last fall, when I was upset because Robbie B. had told me during gym that I was named after a kidnapper.

I had left my keys at school and waited two and a half hours at Belle's Market on Amsterdam Avenue for Mom to get home from work. I didn't mind the waiting so much. I helped Belle out around the store for a while. And I had my book, of course.

"Still reading that same book?" Belle asked, once I had settled into my folding chair next to the cash register to read. "It's looking pretty beat-up."

"I'm not *still* reading it," I told her. "I'm reading it *again*." I had probably read it a hundred times, which was why it looked so beat-up.

"Okay," Belle said, "so let's hear something about this book. What's the first line? I never judge a book by the cover," she said. "I judge by the first line."

I knew the first line of my book without even looking. "It was a dark and stormy night," I said.

She nodded. "Classic. I like that. What's the story about?"

I thought for a second. "It's about a girl named Meg—her dad is missing, and she goes on this trip to another planet to save him."

"And? Does she have a boyfriend?"

"Sort of," I said. "But that's not really the point."

"How old is she?"

"Twelve." The truth is that my book doesn't say how old Meg is, but I am twelve, so she feels twelve to me. When I first got the book I was eleven, and she felt eleven.

"Oh, twelve," Belle said. "Plenty of time for boyfriends, then. Why don't you start from the beginning?"

"Start what from the beginning?"

"The story. Tell me the story. From the beginning."

So I started telling her the story of my book, not reading it to her, just telling her about it, starting with the first scene, where Meg wakes up at night, afraid of a thunderstorm.

While she listened, Belle made me a turkey sandwich and gave me about ten chewable vitamin Cs because she thought I sounded nasal. When she went to the bathroom, I sneaked a little bunch of grapes, which I love but can't ever have, because Mom doesn't like the way the grape pickers are treated in California and she refuses to buy them.

* * *

When she finally got there, Mom hugged Belle and told her, "I owe you," like I was some repulsive burden instead of the person who had very helpfully unpacked three boxes of green bananas and scoured the refrigerated section for expired dairy items. Then Mom bought a box of strawberries, even though I know she thinks Belle's strawberries are overpriced and not very good. She calls them SSO's, which stands for "strawberry-shaped objects."

"Where did Robbie B. get the dumb idea that anyone would name her own daughter after a murderer?" Mom asked. Our building was still half a block away, but her key was already in her hand. Mom doesn't like to fumble around in front of the building looking like a target for muggers.

"Not a murderer," I said. "A kidnapper. Robbie B.'s dad is a prosecutor. He says the Miranda warnings were named for a guy named Mr. Miranda who committed some horrible crime. Is that true?"

"Technically? Maybe. The Miranda warnings are essential, you know. People need to know that they have the right to remain silent and the right to an attorney. What kind of justice system would we have without—"

" 'Maybe' meaning 'yes'?"

"—and then there's Shakespeare. He invented the name Miranda, you know, for *The Tempest*."

It made perfect sense now that I thought about it: Mom wanted to be a criminal defense lawyer—she started law school and almost finished her first year, but then I was born and she had to quit. Now she's a paralegal, except she works at a really small law office where she has to be the receptionist and the secretary too. Richard is one of the lawyers. They do a lot of free work for poor people, sometimes even for criminals. But I never dreamed she would name me after one.

Mom unlocked the lobby door, which is iron and glass and must weigh three hundred pounds, and she pushed hard to swing it open, her heels slipping on the tile floor. When we were inside, she leaned against the other side of the door until she heard the click that means the lock has caught. When the door swings shut by itself, it usually doesn't lock, which drives Mom nuts and is one of the things the landlord won't fix.

"So? Was he a kidnapper or not?" I punched the button for the elevator.

"Okay, you win," Mom said. "I named you after a monster, Mira. I'm sorry. If you don't like your name, you are welcome to change it."

That was so Mom. She didn't understand that a person gets attached to a person's name, that something like this might come as a shock.

Upstairs, she threw her coat on a kitchen chair, filled the spaghetti pot with water, and put it on to boil. She was wearing an orange turtleneck and a denim skirt with purple and black striped tights.

"Nice tights," I snorted. Or I tried to snort, anyway. I'm not exactly sure how, though people in books are always doing it.

She leaned against the sink and flipped through the mail. "You already hassled me about the tights this morning, Mira."

"Oh." She was usually still in bed when I left for school, so I didn't get to appreciate her outfit until she got home from work. "Nice nail polish, then." Her nails were electric blue. She must have done them at her desk that day.

She rolled her eyes. "Are you mad about waiting at Belle's? I was super busy—I couldn't just leave."

"No. I like it at Belle's." I wondered whether she'd done her nails before, after, or during her super busy afternoon.

"You could have gone to Sal's, you know." Sal and his mom, Louisa, live in the apartment below ours. Sal used to be my best friend.

"I said I *like* it at Belle's."

"Still. I think we should hide a key in the fire hose, for the next time."

So after dinner we hid our spare key inside the nozzle of the dusty, folded-up fire hose in the stairwell. The hose is all cracked-looking and about a hundred years old, and Mom always says that if there's an actual fire it will be of no use whatsoever and we'll have to jump out the window into the neighbor's garden. It's a good thing we live on the second floor.

You asked me to mention the key. If I ever do decide to write your letter, which I probably won't, this is the story I would tell you.

The Speed Round

There are two parts to *The $20,000 Pyramid*. Mom calls the first part the speed round because it's all about speed. Contestants try to make their celebrity partners guess seven common words by giving clues. So if the first word is "fork," a contestant might say, "You use this to put food in your mouth—not a spoon but a . . ."

If he has a brain, which Mom says he might not, the celebrity partner will say "Fork!" and then there'll be a ding and the next word will show up on a little hidden screen. Each team gets thirty seconds for seven words.

Then the little screens swivel around, and it's the celebrities' turn to give the clues and the contestants' turn to guess. Another seven words, another thirty seconds. Then the screens swivel back, and the contestants give the clues again.

There are a possible twenty-one points in the speed round, and a perfect score earns a cash bonus of twenty-one hundred dollars. But the most important thing is just to beat the other team, because the team that wins the speed round goes to the Winner's Circle, and the Winner's Circle is where the big money is.

There isn't a lot of time for practice tonight because it's tenant-meeting night. Once a month, the neighbors sit in our living room and complain while Mom takes notes in shorthand. Most people don't bother to come. It's always the old folks, who don't get asked to go many places and are mad that there isn't more heat. Sal's mom, Louisa, works in a nursing home, and she says old people can never get enough heat.

After the meetings, during which Mr. Nunzi has usually burned a new hole in our couch with his cigarette, Mom always writes a letter to the landlord and sends a copy to some city agency that's supposed to care whether we have hot water, if the lobby door locks, and that the elevator keeps getting stuck between floors. But nothing ever changes.

Our doorbell is going to start ringing any minute. Mom is running through a few speed rounds with Richard while I make lemonade from frozen concentrate and open the Oreos.

Louisa knocks her regular knock and I answer the door with the plate of cookies. She takes an Oreo and sighs. She's wearing jeans with her white nurse shoes, which she kicks off by the door. She hates these meetings but comes out of loyalty to Mom. And someone has to watch Mr. Nunzi's cigarette to make sure he doesn't accidentally set our apartment on fire.

"Lemonade?" I ask. I refuse to play waitress during Mom's get-togethers, but I'll pour Louisa a drink anytime.

"Lemonade sounds lovely." She follows me to the kitchen.

Just as I put the glass in her hand, the doorbell buzzes for about a minute straight. Why, why, *why* do they have to hold the button down forever?

"Old people," Louisa says, as if she can read my mind. "They're so used to being ignored." She grabs two more cookies and goes to answer the door. Louisa doesn't normally eat what she calls processed foods, but she says she could never get through a tenant meeting without Oreos.

Fifteen minutes later, Mom is sitting on the living room floor, writing furiously as everyone takes turns saying that the elevator is dirty, there are cigarette butts on the stairs, and the dryer in the basement melted somebody's elastic-waist pants.

I lean against the wall in the hallway and watch her hold up one finger to signal Mrs. Bindocker to slow down. Once Mrs. Bindocker gets going, not even Mom's shorthand can keep up with her.

Mom cried the first time she saw our apartment. The whole place was filthy, she says. The wood floors were "practically black," the windows were "caked with dirt," and the walls were smeared with something she "didn't even want to think about." Always in those same words.

I was there that day—in a little bucket-seat baby carrier. It was cold out, and she had a new coat on. There were no hangers in the closets, and she didn't want to put the coat down on the dirty floor or drape

it over one of the peeling, hissing radiators, so she carried it while she went from room to room, telling herself it wasn't so awful.

At this point in the story, I used to try to think of
someplace she could have put her coat, if only she had
thought of it.

"Why didn't you drape it over the rod in the hall
closet?" I'd ask.

"Dusty," she'd say.

"On the windowsill in the kitchen?"

"Dusty."

"What about over the top of the bedroom door?"

"Couldn't reach," she'd say, "*and* dusty."

What Mom did that day almost twelve years ago
was put her coat back on, pick up my bucket seat, and
walk to a store, where she bought a mop, some soap,
garbage bags, a roll of sticky shelf paper, sponges, a
bottle of window spray, and paper towels.

Back home, she dumped everything out on the
floor. Then she folded her coat and slid it into the
empty bag from the store. She hung the bag on a
doorknob and cleaned the apartment all afternoon. I
knew enough, she says, to snuggle down in my bucket
seat and take a very long nap.

She met Louisa, who didn't have a husband either, in
the lobby on that first day. They were both taking
garbage to the big cans out front. Louisa was holding Sal.
Sal had been crying, but when he saw me, he stopped.

I know all this because I used to ask to hear the
story over and over: the story of the day I met Sal.

Things That Kick

Losing Sal was like a long list of bad things, and somewhere in the top half of the list was the fact that I had to walk home alone past the crazy guy on our corner.

He showed up around the beginning of the school year, when Sal and I still walked home from school together. A few kids called him Quack, short for Quackers, or they called him Kicker because he used to do these sudden kicks into the street, like he was trying to punt one of the cars speeding up Amsterdam Avenue. Sometimes he shook his fist at the sky and yelled crazy stuff like "What's the burn scale? Where's the dome?" and then he threw his head back and laughed these loud, crazy laughs, so everyone could see that he had about thirty fillings in his teeth. And he was always on our corner, sometimes sleeping with his head under the mailbox.

"Don't call him Quack," Mom said. "That's an awful name for a human being."

"Even a human being who's quackers?"

"I don't care. It's still awful."

"Well, what do *you* call him?"

"I don't call him anything," she said, "but I think of him as the laughing man."

Back when I still walked home with Sal, it was easier to pretend that the laughing man didn't scare me, because Sal was pretending too. He tried not to show it, but he freaked when he saw the laughing man shaking his fist at the sky and kicking his leg out into traffic. I could tell by the way Sal's face kind of froze. I know all of his expressions.

I used to think of Sal as being a part of me: Sal and Miranda, Miranda and Sal. I knew he wasn't really, but that's the way it felt.

When we were too little for school, Sal and I went to day care together at a lady's apartment down the block. She had picked up some carpet samples at a store on Amsterdam Avenue and written the kids' names on the backs. After lunch, she'd pass out these carpet squares and we'd pick our spots on the living room floor for nap time. Sal and I always lined ours up to make a rectangle.

One time, when Sal had a fever and Louisa had called in sick to her job and kept him home, the day-care lady handed me my carpet square at nap time, and then, a second later, she gave me Sal's, too.

"I know how it is, baby," she said.

And then I lay on her floor not sleeping because Sal wasn't there to press his foot against mine.

* * *

When he first showed up on our corner last fall, the laughing man was always mumbling under his breath. "Bookbag, pocketshoe, bookbag, pocketshoe."

He said it like a chant: *bookbag, pocketshoe, bookbag, pocketshoe.* And sometimes he would be hitting himself on the head with his fists. Sal and I usually tried to get really interested in our conversation and act like we didn't notice. It's crazy the things a person can pretend not to notice.

"Why do you think he sleeps like that, with his head under the mailbox?" I asked Richard back when the laughing man was brand-new and I was still trying to figure him out.

"I don't know," Richard said, looking up from the paper. "Maybe so nobody steps on his head?"

"Very funny. And what's a 'pocketshoe,' anyway?"

"Pocketshoe," he said, looking serious. "Noun: An extra shoe you keep in your pocket. In case someone steals one of yours while you're asleep with your head under the mailbox."

"Ha ha ha," I said.

"Oh, Mr. Perfect," Mom said. "You and your amazing dictionary head!" She was in one of her good moods that day.

Richard tapped his right knee and went back to his newspaper.

Things That Get Tangled

Lucky for Mom, some of the old people at the nursing home where Louisa works like to watch *The $20,000 Pyramid* at lunchtime. Louisa takes notes on every show and brings them over after work. She gets off at four, so I have time to write out the day's words on stolen index cards before Mom gets home.

Tonight, Mom and Richard are practicing in the living room. I'm supposed to be doing homework in my room, but instead I'm tying knots and I'm thinking.

It was Richard who taught me how to tie knots. He learned back when he sailed boats as a kid, and he still carries pieces of rope in his briefcase. He says that when he's trying to solve a problem at work, he takes out the ropes, ties them into knots, unties them, and then ties them again. It gets him in the right frame of mind.

Two Christmases ago, which was his first Christmas with us, Richard gave me my own set of ropes and started showing me knots. Now I can make every knot he knows, even the clove hitch, which I did backward for a few months before I got it right. So I am tying and untying knots, and seeing if it helps me solve my problem, which is you. I have no idea what you expect from me.

If you just wanted to know what happened that day this past winter, it would be easy. Not fun, but easy. But that's not what your note says. It says to write down the story of what happened *and everything that led up to it.* And, as Mom likes to say, that's a whole different bucket of poop. Except she doesn't use the word "poop."

Because even if you were still here, even if I *did* decide to write the letter, I wouldn't know where to start. The day the laughing man showed up on our corner? The day Mom and Louisa met in the lobby? The day I found your first note?

There is no answer. But if someone sat on my legs and forced me to name the day the whole true story began, I'd say it was the day Sal got punched.

Things That Stain

It happened in the fall, when Sal and I still walked home from school together every single day: one block from West End Avenue to Broadway, one block from Broadway to Amsterdam, past the laughing man on our corner, and then half a block to our lobby door.

That middle block between Broadway and Amsterdam is mostly a huge garage, where the sidewalk is all slanted, and we had to be careful when it was icy or else we'd slip right in front of the pack of boys always hanging out there. If we did fall, they'd make a really big deal out of it, staggering around laughing, and sometimes calling us names that made our hearts beat fast the rest of the way home.

The day Sal got punched, there was no ice on the ground because it was only October. I was carrying the big oak-tag *Mysteries of Science* poster I'd made at school. I had drawn big bubble letters for the title, which was *Why Do We Yawn?*

There are a lot of interesting theories about yawning. Some people think it started as a way of showing off the teeth to scare predators away, or as a way to stretch facial muscles, or to signal to the rest of the tribe that it's time to sleep. My own theory, which I included on my poster, is that yawning is a semipolite way of telling someone that they're boring everyone to death. Either that or it's a slow-motion sneeze. But no one knows for sure, which is why it's a mystery of science.

The day Sal got punched, the boys by the garage were hanging out, as usual. The day before, there had been a fight, with one of them slamming another one up against a parked car and hitting him. The kid getting hit had both his hands up like he was saying "Enough!", but every time he tried to get off the hood of that car, the other kid pushed him down and hit him again. The other boys were all jumping around and yelling and Sal and I had crossed to the other side of the street so that we wouldn't get accidentally slammed by somebody.

On the day Sal got punched, the boys were being regular, so we stayed on our usual side. But just as we started past the garage, someone moved away from the group. He took a big step toward me and Sal and blocked our way so that we had to stop. I looked up and saw a not-too-biggish kid in a green army coat. He made a fist that came up like a wave and hit Sal right in the stomach. Hard. Sal doubled over and gurgled like he was going to throw up. And then the kid whacked him across the face.

"Sal!" I yelled. I glanced over at Belle's Market on

Amsterdam, but no one was out front. Sal was bent over and frozen. The kid just stood there for a few seconds with his head tilted to one side. It seemed crazy, but it actually looked like he was reading my *Mysteries of Science* poster. Then he turned away and started strolling toward Broadway like nothing had happened.

"Sal!" I leaned over to see his face, which looked okay but had one cheek all red. "Walk," I said. "We're almost home."

Sal's feet started to move. It took me a few steps to realize that the boys weren't laughing or whistling or calling us names. They hadn't made a sound. I looked back and saw them standing there, staring after the kid in the green army coat, who was still walking in the other direction.

"Hey!" one of them yelled down the block after him. "What the hell was that?" But the kid didn't look back.

Sal was moving slowly. He squeezed the arms of the blue satin Yankees jacket Louisa got him for his birthday, and tears were dropping down his face, and I almost cried but didn't. It was my job to get him home, and we still had to get by the laughing man.

He was on our corner, marching around in a circle and doing some salutes. Sal was crying harder and walking in a hunch. Some blood had started dripping out of his nose, and he wiped it with the blue and white striped cuff of his jacket. He gagged a lot. It sounded like he really might throw up.

When he saw us, the laughing man dropped his arms to his sides and stood up straight. He reminded me of the big wooden nutcracker Louisa puts out on her kitchen table at Christmastime.

"Smart kid!" he said. He took a step toward us, and it was enough to make Sal take off running for home. I ran after him, trying to hold on to my poster and get my keys out of my jeans.

When I had gotten us into the lobby, Sal went straight to his apartment and closed the door on me. I knocked for a while, but Louisa wasn't home from work yet and he wouldn't let me in.

If I'm not wrong, this is the beginning of the story you wanted me to tell. And I didn't know it yet, but it was also the end of my friendship with Sal.

Mom's Rules for Life in New York City

1. *Always* have your key out before you reach the front door.
2. If a stranger is hanging out in front of the building, don't *ever* go in—just keep walking around the block until he's gone.
3. Look ahead. If there's someone acting strange down the block, looking drunk or dangerous, cross to the other side of the street, but *don't* be obvious about it. Make it look like you were planning to cross the street all along.
4. *Never* show your money on the street.

I have my own trick. If I'm afraid of someone on the street, I'll turn to him (it's always a boy) and say, "Excuse me, do you happen to know what time it is?" This is my way of saying to the person, "I see you as a friend, and there is no need to hurt me or take my

stuff. Also, I don't even have a watch and I am probably not worth mugging."

So far, it's worked like gangbusters, as Richard
would say. And I've discovered that most people I'm
afraid of are actually very friendly.

Things You Wish For

"Miranda?" Mom calls from the kitchen. "We need you to keep time. This egg-timer ticking is driving me crazy."

So I watch the second hand of the kitchen clock while Richard feeds Mom clues. Then Mom gives the clues while Richard guesses.

"Can I play?" I ask after about five rounds.

"Sure. Richard, you keep time for a while." Mom stretches and peels off her purple sweatshirt. As it goes over her head, her hair falls free of the collar and bounces down around her shoulders. As usual, this makes me curse my nonexistent dad, who must be to blame for my hair, which is straight, brown, and just kind of *there*. I blame this stupid flat brown hair on my father, but otherwise I don't hold any grudges against him.

In my book, Meg is looking for her father. When she finally gets to Camazotz, which is a planet somewhere near the Big Dipper where he's being held prisoner, this evil man with red eyes asks her *why* she wants him, and she says, "Didn't you ever have a father yourself? You don't want him for a *reason*. You want him because he's your *father*."

So I figure it's because I never *had* a father that I don't want one now. A person can't miss something she never had.

Richard is looking at the kitchen clock, waiting for the second hand to get to the twelve. "Okay, get ready—go!"

I look down at the first card. "Um, this is something you spread on toast," I say.

"Butter!" Mom yells.

Next card. "You drink a milk shake with this, you suck through it."

"A straw!" Mom yells.

Next. "It's leather and it holds your pants up!"

"A belt!"

"It's sweet—you drink it in winter, after you go sledding!"

"Hot chocolate!"

It's good to play, to think of nothing but the next word and to have Mom think of nothing but the next words out of my mouth. We fly through the pack of seven words.

"You're good at this," Mom says when we finish with five seconds to spare.

I'm smiling. "I really think you're going to win," I tell her.

"Don't get your hopes up," she warns. "This is just the speed round. The speed round is the easy part."

The truth is that our hopes are already up. Our wish list is stuck to the fridge with a magnet Mom stole from work:

> *Trip to China*
> *Good camera for trip to China*
> *Wall-to-wall carpeting for Miranda's room*
> *New TV*

And Richard has scribbled *Sailboat* at the bottom, though it's hard to imagine where we would park it.

That's the official list, anyway. Richard and I have our own secret plan for the money, if Mom wins it.

Things That Sneak Up on You

The day Sal got punched, back in October, Louisa came upstairs after dinner to have a conference with Mom in her bedroom. They decided that Sal needed a mental health day, which meant he was allowed to skip school and watch TV the next day.

So the following afternoon I walked home alone. I was doing a lot of talking in my head so that I would be deep in conversation with myself by the time I got to the laughing man. I was almost to the garage when I realized someone was walking right behind me. I glanced back and saw the kid who punched Sal. He was maybe two feet away, wearing the same green army jacket he had worn the day before.

I was about to panic. I always know when I'm about to panic because my knees and neck both start to tingle. And then, before I had really decided what to do, I turned around to face him.

"Excuse me, do you happen to know what time it is?" My voice sounded almost normal. That was good.

"Let's see. . . ." He turned his head and looked back toward Broadway like maybe there was a giant clock hovering in the air right behind us. "It's three-sixteen."

I nodded like I could see the invisible clock too. "Thanks." He didn't look like he was about to hit me, but still, my heart was pounding.

He pointed. "See that big brown building? Yesterday the sun started to go behind it at three-twelve. Now it's about halfway gone." He glanced at me. "Plus, it's one day later, and it's October, so the days are getting shorter."

I stared at him. He looked down at his hand, which held a key. He pushed the other hand into his pants pocket. "I don't have a watch," he said.

"Oh," I said. "Me neither."

He nodded, and I wasn't afraid anymore. But as soon as the fear was gone, I filled up with guilt. "Look at you," my brain said, "chatting with the kid who punched Sal!" My brain has a way of talking to me like that.

"I've got to go," I said, and I didn't let myself glance back until I got to the corner. When I did, the kid who punched Sal was gone. That was when I realized that he must live in the apartment over the garage, the one with dead plants on the fire escape and bedsheets hanging over the windows.

I'd forgotten all about the laughing man. His legs were sticking out from under the mailbox, and I was careful not to wake him.

Things That Bounce

After he got punched, Sal started playing basketball in the alley behind our building. Our living room windows face that way, and I heard him dribbling his ball back there from about three-thirty to five every day. There was a rusted-out metal hoop with no net that made a clanging sound whenever he hit it.

Sal and Louisa's apartment is mostly the same as ours. We have the same rectangular bedrooms, the same pull-chain light in the hallway, the same weird-shaped kitchen with the same unpredictable ovens, theirs right below ours.

There are differences. Their kitchen floor is yellow and orange linoleum squares instead of the white with gold flakes that we have, and Sal's bed is up against a different wall in the bedroom. But we have the same bathroom floor—these white hexagonal tiles. If I look at them long enough, I can see all kinds of patterns in those hexagons: lines, arrows, even flowers. They kind of shift into these different pictures. It's the sort of thing a person would never try to explain to anyone else, but once, when we were little, I told Sal about it, and then we went into his bathroom to stare at the floor together. Sal and Miranda, Miranda and Sal.

Sal played basketball more and more and talked to me less and less. I asked him four hundred times whether he was okay, or if he was mad at me, or what was wrong, and three hundred and ninety-nine times he answered "Yes," "No," and "Nothing." Then, the last time I asked, he told me, while standing in our lobby and looking at his feet, that he didn't want to have lunch or walk home together for a while.

"Do you even want to be friends at all?" I asked him.

He glared at his feet and said no, he guessed he didn't for a while.

I was lucky, I guess, that this was the same week Julia decided to punish Annemarie for something.

The girls at school had been hurting each other's feelings for years before Sal left me and I was forced to really notice them. I had watched them trade best friends, start wars, cry, trade back, make treaties, squeal and grab each other's arms in this fake-excited way, et cetera, et cetera. I had seen which ones tortured Alice Evans, who, even though we'd started *sixth grade,* still waited too long to pee and never wanted to say out loud that she had to go. These girls would wait until Alice was pretty far gone, jiggling one foot and then the other, and then they would start asking her questions. "Alice," they'd say, "did you do today's page in the math workbook yet? Where it says 'multiply to check your answer'? How did you do that?" And she'd desperately hop around while showing them.

I knew the way the girls all paired up, and Julia and Annemarie had been paired up for a long time. Julia I hated. Annemarie I had never thought about much.

My first memory of Julia is from second grade, when we made self-portraits in art. She complained there was no "café au lait"–colored construction paper for her skin, or "sixty-percent-cacao-chocolate" color for her eyes. I remember staring at her while these words came out of her mouth, and thinking, Your skin is light brown. Your eyes are dark brown. Why don't you just use brown, you idiot? Jay Stringer didn't complain about the paper, and neither did any of the other ten kids using brown. I didn't complain about the stupid hot-pink color I'd been given. Did my skin look hot-pink to her?

But I soon found out that Julia wasn't like the rest of us. She took trips all over the world with her parents. She would disappear from school and show up two weeks later with satin ribbons worked into her braids, or with a new green velvet scoop-neck dress, or wearing three gold rings on one finger. She learned about sixty-percent-cacao chocolate, she said, in Switzerland, where her parents had bought her a lot of it, along with a little silver watch she was always shoving in people's faces.

* * *

I still don't know what Annemarie did wrong, but during silent reading period that Tuesday, Julia told her that, as punishment, she wasn't going to have lunch with Annemarie for "the remainder of the week." Julia was big on announcing things in a loud voice so that everyone could hear. So on Wednesday, I asked Annemarie if she wanted to go out to lunch with me and she said yes.

In sixth grade, kids with any money, even just a little, go out for lunch unless something is going on and they won't let us, like the first week of school, when there was a man running down Broadway stark naked and we all had to eat in the school cafeteria while the police tried to catch him.

Mostly kids go to the pizza place, or to McDonald's, or, every once in a while, to the sandwich place, which has a real name but which we called Jimmy's because there was never anyone working there except one guy called Jimmy.

Pizza is the best deal—a dollar fifty will buy two slices, a can of soda, and a cherry Blow Pop from the candy bucket next to the register. That first day together, Annemarie and I got lucky and found two stools next to each other at the counter under the flag of Italy.

I found it slightly gross to eat pizza with Annemarie because she peeled the cheese off her slice like a scab and ate it, leaving everything else on her plate.

But she laughed at my jokes (which I mostly stole from Richard, who is bad at telling jokes but knows a lot of them), and she invited me over to her house after school, which more than made up for it. I would be spared an afternoon of listening to Sal's basketball. And the laughing man might be asleep under his mailbox by the time I walked home.

Things That Burn

Annemarie's apartment didn't involve keys. Instead she had a doorman who slapped her five and a dad who opened the door upstairs.

"Did your dad take the day off?" I whispered.

"No," Annemarie said, "he works from home. He illustrates medical journals."

"Is your mom here too?"

She shook her head. "She's at work."

Annemarie's bedroom was about the same size as mine, but it had nice curtains and the walls were completely covered with all kinds of pictures and photographs, which I couldn't stop looking at. There must have been a hundred of them.

"We've known each other for a long time," Annemarie said, sitting down on her bed, which had some kind of Asian bedspread and about fifty pillows on it.

"Who?"

She blushed. "Oh—I thought you were looking at the pictures of Julia."

That's when I noticed that her room was covered

with pictures of Julia. Maybe not covered, exactly, but there were a lot of them—the two of them in pajamas, or in the park, or standing together all dressed up outside some theater.

"Knock, knock!" Annemarie's dad came in with these tiny sausages on a plate. "I'm on deadline," he said to me. "When I'm on deadline, I cook. Do you like mustard? Try the dipping sauce. I'll be right back with some apple cider."

He was back in thirty seconds with a glass of cider for me, but he handed Annemarie what looked like plain water. She didn't seem to notice.

Annemarie's rug was spongy and soft, almost like another bed, and I lay down on it. Mustard always makes my lips burn, but I didn't care. It was worth it.

The Winner's Circle

Mom is getting very good at the speed round. She almost always gets seven words in thirty seconds now, no matter who is giving the clues and who is guessing.

The second part of *The $20,000 Pyramid* is called the Winner's Circle because you have to win the speed round to get there. In the Winner's Circle, the celebrity partner gives the clues and the contestant has to guess—not words, but categories. So if the celebrity says "tulip, daisy, rose," the contestant would say "types of flowers."

That's an easy one. Some of the categories are harder to figure out, like "things you recite" (poetry, the Pledge of Allegiance) or "things you squeeze" (a tube of toothpaste, someone's hand).

The last category is always incredibly hard to guess—maybe "things you prolong" or "things that are warped." The last category is what stands between the contestants and the big money, and Mom says it doesn't help that some of these celebrity partners are as dumb as a bag of hair.

If Mom wins her first speed round and correctly

guesses all the categories in the Winner's Circle, she'll win ten thousand dollars. If she wins a second speed round, the Winner's Circle is worth fifteen thousand dollars. And if she wins a third time, she'll go for twenty thousand dollars. That's what I mean by big money.

During the speed round, you can point or gesture all you want. If the word is "nose," you can point to your nose. But the rules change in the Winner's Circle. No hand movements of any kind are allowed, which is why I'm tying Richard's arms to my desk chair. I'm using the clove hitch.

"You've got it reversed again," Richard says, watching me. "That end should go *through* the loop. . . . *That's* it—right!"

Mom is looking at us like we're crazy. "Is this really necessary?"

"She has to practice," he tells her. "For when you win the sailboat."

Mom rolls her eyes.

I get my cards ready—I've written everything out in fat block letters so Richard can read them from a distance. I'm going to hold them up one at a time behind Mom's head, where Richard can see them. In the real show, they have these big panels that spin around behind the contestant's head to reveal the next category, but obviously we don't have that kind of technology.

Louisa's lunchtime notes are good—she's even written down what Dick Clark says at the beginning of every Winner's Circle. He always uses the same words: "Here is your first subject. . . . Go."

We set the egg timer for one minute. Mom has to guess the names of six categories before it goes off. "Here is your first subject," I say, trying to sound like Dick Clark. "Go." I hold up the first card so Richard can see it.

The card says "things you climb." Richard nods and starts giving Mom clues.

"A jungle gym, a mountain . . ."

"High things?" Mom guesses.

Richard shakes his head. "Um . . . stairs . . ."

"Things that go up!" she yells.

He shakes his head again. ". . . a ladder . . ."

"Things you climb!"

"Ding!" I say, and hold up the next card.

"Okay," Richard says. "Paris, cheese, wine . . ."

"Fancy things!" Mom yells. "Romantic things!"

". . . fries . . ."

"French things!"

"Ding!" Next card.

"A pillow," Richard says. "A kitten."

"Soft things?"

". . . a cotton ball . . ."

"Puffy things—fluffy things!"

"Ding!" Next card.

"A baby carriage, a shopping cart . . ."

"Things that carry things?" Mom guesses. "Things with wheels?"

Richard shakes his head, thinks, and says, "A button."

"Things you push!"

"Ding!"

The egg timer goes off. We all look at each other—Mom has only guessed four of the six categories. No one says anything.

"It's okay," Mom says finally. "We still have two more weeks."

Things You Keep Secret

It was a while before I realized that the kid who punched Sal went to our school. We were working on our projects for Main Street, which is a scale model of a city block that we're constructing in the back of our classroom. Mr. Tompkin's class studies buildings every year. Mom says he's a frustrated architect.

"Why is he frustrated?" I asked.

"It's complicated." She said it had to do with the war. "Teachers didn't have to go fight in Vietnam. So a lot of young men who didn't want to fight became teachers."

Instead of what they really wanted to be, she meant.

Jay Stringer, who is a twelve-year-old genius and the head of the Main Street Planning Board, had already built an entire cardboard building, complete with fire escapes and a water tower, and he'd just started two phone booths that he said would have tiny doors that folded open and closed.

Annemarie was busy with her pebbles and her

extra-strength glue, working on a stone wall for the park that Jay Stringer had approved the week before. Julia was making a tinfoil UFO that she said would fly up and down the street on an invisible wire. The UFO hadn't been approved yet, but Julia was going ahead with it anyway. She had written *Proposal Pending* on a piece of paper and taped it to the end of a shoe box full of foil and fishing line. Alice Evans was trying to make fire hydrants out of clay, which so far just looked like pathetic lumps. Having to pee so badly all the time must have made it hard for her to concentrate.

I worked on the diagrams for my playground proposal. My slide looked too steep, and then too flat, and then too messy, because I had erased so much. I would have to ask for another sheet of graph paper, which always made Jay Stringer sigh and roll his eyes, because he brought it from home.

The classroom phone rang, and after he answered it, Mr. Tompkin asked if anyone wanted to go be an office monitor for a while. I raised my hand. The school secretary usually gives office monitors a few Bit-O-Honeys or Hershey's Kisses.

I grabbed my book and rode the banisters down to the first floor, where I found Wheelie at her desk in the main office. She's called the secretary, but as far as I can tell she basically runs the school. And she tries to do it without getting out of her desk chair, which has wheels, which is why everyone calls her Wheelie. She rolls herself around the office all day by pushing off the floor with her feet. It's like pinball in slow motion.

"The dentist needs a runner," she said to me, kicking herself over to a desk, where she picked up a sheet of paper.

It's weird to go to a school for almost seven years and then one day discover that there's a dentist's office inside it. But that is exactly what happened. Wheelie stood up, and I followed her out of the office and around the corner to a short dead-end hallway I had never thought about before. There was one open door, and on the other side of it was a real dentist's office.

We walked into a waiting area, and I could see into another room with a regular dentist's chair. It had a little white sink attached, and one of those big silver lights over it. The walls were covered with posters about eating apples and plaque and brushing your teeth.

Wheelie called out "Bruce?" and a guy with a short gray beard popped his head into the waiting room. He was wearing one of those green doctor tops and he gave me a big perfect smile.

"Hey there. Are you my first appointment?"

"No, this is Miranda," Wheelie said. "She's your runner. I have the patient list right here." And she handed me the piece of paper.

I saw a bunch of names and classroom numbers. "They go to the dentist at school?" I said. "That's so weird."

Wheelie snatched back the paper and said, "There

are ninety-eight sixth graders in this school. Eighty-nine of them are in attendance today, so if you can't do this politely, you can go straight back to your classroom and I'll find another one for the job."

I felt my face go hot and actually thought I might cry. Sometimes when I'm caught off guard I cry at almost nothing.

The dentist put a hand on my shoulder and smiled again. He was like a professional smiler, which makes sense for a dentist, I guess. "My services don't cost anything, Miranda. Some families don't have the money to pay a dentist. Or they could really use the money for something else."

"Oh." I was thinking I shouldn't let my mother find out about this. She's always complaining about how health care should be free for everyone. I bet she would have me signed up for the dentist at school in no time.

The dentist looked at Wheelie, and she forced a little smile and handed me the list again. Then she fished a warm Bit-O-Honey out of her pocket and gave it to me right there in front of the dentist, even though Louisa had once told me that you might as well whack your own teeth with a wrench as eat Bit-O-Honeys.

I set out with my list. "Don't get the kids all at once," the dentist called after me. "Bring them in twos."

I decided to get the little kids first. I knocked on

their classroom doors and their teachers came hurrying to see my note, and the kids were handed over to me. I walked the two kindergartners to the dentist's office, read my book in the waiting room for a while, and then went back for a second grader and a fourth grader. It was a lot of climbing up and down stairs. Not in a million years could I imagine Wheelie doing this.

When I got back to the dentist with my second drop, one of the kindergartners was already waiting to go back to class. She had this big smiley-tooth sticker on her shirt. I brought her back to her classroom and then went for the last kid on my list, a sixth grader like me: Marcus Heilbroner, in class 6-506. I'd never heard of him.

I knocked on the little window in the classroom door, waving my paper. The teacher, Mr. Anderson, came over, and I showed him my list.

"Marcus," he called, and a boy stood up.

It was the boy who hit Sal. He'd gotten a very short haircut, but he was definitely the same person. My brain started yelling at me: "It's the kid who hit Sal! He goes to your *school*? The kid who hit Sal goes to your *school*?" And meanwhile, the kid had walked over to where I was standing with Mr. Anderson.

"Dentist appointment," Mr. Anderson whispered. Marcus nodded, went back to his desk, picked up a book, and then walked right past me and out the door. I followed a few steps behind him. He knew the way.

* * *

"Welcome back, Marcus," the dentist called from the exam room. "Nice haircut."

The fourth grader was in the big chair, spitting into the little white sink. The other two kids were all stickered up and waiting to go back to class. Marcus sat down heavily and opened his book, which was called *Concepts in Mathematics*.

Mr. Tompkin acted like everyone in our class was part of one big happy math group, but it didn't take much to figure out there was a system: red math books for genius kids like Jay Stringer, orange ones for kids like me who did okay, and yellow ones for kids who left the room twice a week to meet with Ms. Dudley, who did "math support." Marcus's book was different—thick, with a hard cover and small type. So I guessed that even though it was blue—even farther down the rainbow than yellow—it was at least the equivalent of a red.

"You like math, huh?" I said.

He looked up, and I got the strong feeling he didn't know he had ever seen me before, that he didn't remember punching Sal or talking to me about the sun.

"Yeah," he said slowly, like I might be stupid or something. "I like math." And he went back to reading.

I delivered the two waiting kids back to their classes. One of them was holding a shiny paper card shaped like an apple that said she needed a follow-up visit. There was a line for her mom to sign. "Cavity," I thought grimly.

When I got back to the dentist's office, the fourth grader was still in the chair and Marcus was still reading his math book. That was fine with me—I grabbed my book from the table where I'd left it and settled back to read.

"Some people think it's possible, you know," Marcus mumbled.

"What?"

He pointed at my book. "Time travel. Some people think it's possible. Except those ladies lied, at the beginning of the book."

"What?"

"Those ladies in the book—Mrs. What, Mrs. Where, and Mrs. Who."

"Mrs. Whatsit, Mrs. Who, and Mrs. *Which*," I corrected him.

He shrugged.

"What do you mean, they lied? They never lied." I was getting annoyed. The truth is that I hate to think about other people reading my book. It's like watching someone go through the box of private stuff that I keep under my bed.

"Don't you remember?" He leaned forward in his chair. "They're traveling through time, right? All over the universe, right? And they promise that girl that they'll have her back home five minutes before she left. But they don't."

"How do *you* know they don't get her home five minutes before she left? I mean, there's no clock or anything. They leave at night and they get back the same night. Maybe they left at eight-thirty and got home at eight-twenty-five."

He laughed. "You don't need a *clock*. Think. At the beginning of the book, that girl walks through the vegetable garden—"

"Meg."

"Huh?"

"You keep saying 'that girl.' Her name is Meg."

"—so she walks to the far side of the vegetable garden and sits on this stone wall, right? So, she can *see* the garden from where she's sitting and talking with that boy, right? And then those ladies show up and take them away."

"His name is Calvin. And so what if they can see the garden?"

"So the *garden* is where they appear when they get back home at the end of the book. Remember? They land in the broccoli. So if they *had* gotten home five minutes before they left, like those ladies *promised* they would, then they would have seen themselves get back. Before they left."

I put my book down and shook my head. "Think about it. They hadn't even left yet. How could they have gotten back already? They didn't even know for sure whether they *would* get back."

"It doesn't matter whether they knew it. That's got nothing to do with it." He leaned back and shoved his hands in his pockets. "If they land in the broccoli at eight-twenty-five, they should be in the broccoli at eight-twenty-five. Period."

"That makes no sense," I said. "What if they couldn't do it—save Meg's father and get back in one piece?"

"Then they wouldn't have landed in the broccoli at all. But they did do it, right?"

"Yes, but—the end can't happen before the middle!"

He smiled. "Why can't it?"

"I don't know—it's common sense!"

"Common sense! Have you read *Relativity*? You know—by Einstein?"

I glared at him.

"Einstein says common sense is just habit of thought. It's how we're *used* to thinking about things, but a lot of the time it just gets in the way."

"In the way of *what*?"

"In the way of what's true. I mean, it used to be common sense that the world was flat and the sun revolved around it. But at some point, someone had to reject that assumption, or at least question it."

"Well, obviously somebody did."

"Well, *duh*. Copernicus did! Look, all I'm saying is that at the end of the book, they don't get back five minutes before they left. Or they would have seen themselves get back—before they left."

I gave up. "It was dark in the garden," I said. "Maybe they just couldn't see themselves from where they were sitting."

"I thought of that," he said. "But they would have heard all the yelling, and the dog—"

"My God, what does it *matter*? It's a *story*—someone made it up! You do realize that, don't you?"

He shrugged. "The story is made up. But time travel is possible. In theory. I've read some articles about it."

"Wow. You really *do* like math, don't you?"

He smiled again. With his supershort hair, his head looked like a perfectly round ball when he smiled. "This is more like physics."

"Fine. You really like *physics*, don't you?"

"Yeah." He picked up my book from the table and flipped through it. "Actually, I had almost this same conversation with my teacher right after I read this. She didn't understand me at first either."

"She? Mr. Anderson is a *he*. You really don't notice much about people, do you?"

"Not Mr. Anderson. This was in second grade. I wrote a book report about it."

"In second grade?"

He put the book down. "Yeah. Back in Detroit, where we used to live, till last year. But I don't talk about this kind of stuff anymore. Usually."

"Why not?"

He shot me a look. "People don't want to think about it."

"I can see why," I said. "It makes my head hurt."

"Still, you did better than most people. You're a pretty smart kid."

I rolled my eyes. "Gee, thanks."

"Okay, Marcus," the dentist chirped from the other room. "You're up!"

I watched Marcus slip into the big chair and begin to read his math book again, holding it up with one hand while the dentist worked from the other side. The fourth grader waited for me by the door with his sticker on.

"Miranda, you can go on back to your class," the dentist called. "Marcus is going to be here awhile. He can walk himself upstairs when we're through."

So I picked up my book and hiked back up the stairs with the fourth grader. As we started down the hallway to his classroom, he stopped, and I waited while he peeled the sticker off his shirt, folded it, and stuck it in his pocket.

Things That Smell

For a long time, Colin was just this short kid who seemed to end up in my class every year. In third grade, he and I spent about a week convincing Alice Evans that velour was a kind of animal fur, and she refused to wear it for the rest of the year. But aside from that, we had never hung out together. I'd seen him with his skateboard in the park a few times, and he always let me have a turn on it, but that was all.

And then suddenly he was everywhere. He came downstairs with me and Annemarie at lunch, or yelled "Hold up" and walked to Broadway with us after school to get drinks at Jimmy's sandwich shop.

It was Colin who had the idea to ask Jimmy for a job. I'm pretty sure he was kidding. Colin was always saying weird stuff to people that made you partly proud to know him and partly wish you weren't standing next to him. Attention-seeking, is what Mom would call him.

"Hey," Colin said to Jimmy after school one day in the beginning of November, when we were paying for our Cokes. "You're always alone in here. How about talking to the owner about giving us jobs?"

"I'm the owner," Jimmy said. "And who's 'us'?"

It was me, Annemarie, and Colin standing there. "Us," Colin said. "We could work after school."

Jimmy grabbed a pickle chunk out of the setup tray, which I didn't know the name of yet, and tossed it into his mouth. "I don't need help that late. What about when I open up?"

"We have lunch at ten-forty-five," Colin said. A stupidly early lunch. At our school, the older you get, the stupider your lunch period.

Jimmy nodded. "That works."

I didn't think Jimmy was serious, but Colin said we should show up at lunchtime the next day, just in case.

And it turned out he was serious. The three of us worked during lunch for the rest of that week. We washed a lot of greasy plastic trays, weighed piles of sliced meat (which is as gross as it sounds), stacked up sodas in the refrigerated case, cut tomatoes, and did whatever else Jimmy said to do.

I guess it's obvious that Jimmy was kind of weird, because no normal person would have given forty-minute-a-day jobs to three sixth graders. On our first day, Jimmy spent about five entire minutes pointing to a plastic bank shaped like Fred Flintstone that he had up on a shelf in the back room. "Never touch the bank," he said. "Never."

When I pointed Jimmy's weirdness out to Annemarie, she said, "Yeah, but he's nice-weird, not creepy-weird."

"You think?" I said. "What about the creepy cartoon bank?"

She shrugged. "My dad collects stuff like that too. Lots of people do."

It turned out that Jimmy didn't intend to pay us any money. Instead, he let us each pick a soda from the refrigerator and make a sandwich from the stuff in the setup tray on the counter. The setup tray was just lettuce, tomato, onions, American cheese, Swiss cheese, and pickles. The other food—sliced turkey, ham, roast beef, and salami, a big tub of tuna salad, and meatballs in a plug-in pot—was off-limits.

Every day, we took our cheese sandwiches back to school and ate them at our desks during silent reading period. I sat next to Alice Evans, who never complained about anything, and Annemarie sat next to Jay Stringer, who was oblivious to the world when he was reading, but Colin sat next to Julia.

"Mr. Tompkin!" Julia said on the Friday of our first week at Jimmy's. "Colin is eating his lunch at his desk *again*. And I *despise* the smell of pickles."

Mr. Tompkin looked up over the top of his book, adjusted his toothpick, and said, "Try breathing through your mouth."

Things You Don't Forget

Our apartment door was unlocked when I got home from school that Friday, which was strange. More than strange, actually—it had never happened before. But I figured Mom had probably just forgotten to lock it when she left for work that morning. It sounds stupid now that I say it, but that's what I thought.

Once I was inside, though, I had this sudden fear that I wasn't alone in the apartment. I dropped my knapsack in the hall and ran down to Sal's. He came to the door but opened it just enough to squeeze his body into the crack.

"My door was unlocked," I said. "Doesn't that seem weird?"

"Yeah," he said. "Maybe you forgot to lock it?" He stayed there wedged into the doorway. Definitely not inviting me in.

"Yeah, probably." I could hear the television behind him, blaring a commercial.

"Okay." He looked up at the ceiling behind me.

I felt like an idiot. "Okay. See you later."

I went back upstairs, made myself a bowl of Cheerios with an inch of sugar on top, and turned on the television. Mom walked in around six.

"You forgot to lock the door this morning," I said.

"What? No, I didn't."

"Well, it wasn't locked when I got home today."

"It wasn't?" She started walking from room to room, opening drawers and closet doors, and I followed her.

"It can't be," she said. "I would never forget to lock the door."

Nothing seemed out of place. She got to the kitchen and stopped. "I guess I don't specifically *remember* locking it, but I know I would never *not* lock it. . . ."

She filled the spaghetti pot with water, and we talked about other stuff while she set the table and I peeled some carrots, but every once in a while she would interrupt herself to say, "How could I have forgotten to lock the door?"

We were halfway through dinner when she suddenly stood up and walked out of the apartment.

"Mom?"

I found her standing in the stairwell, peering into the nozzle of the fire hose. "I knew it," she said. "I would never forget to lock the door. Never."

The key was gone. We searched every room all over again but couldn't find a single thing missing.

"It makes no sense," Mom said, standing over her

jewelry box and staring down at the gold bracelets that had belonged to her mother. "Why steal the key, unlock the door, and not take anything?"

That was Friday afternoon. I found your first note Monday morning.

The First Note

Your first note was written in tiny words on a little square of stiff paper that felt like it had once gotten wet. I was packing my knapsack for school when I noticed it sticking out of my library book—which was about a village of squirrels, or maybe it was mice. I had not bothered to read it.

> M,
>
> This is hard. Harder than I expected, even with your help. But I have been practicing, and my preparations go well. I am coming to save your friend's life, and my own.
>
> I ask two favors.
>
> First, you must write me a letter.
>
> Second, please remember to mention the location of your house key.
>
> The trip is a difficult one. I will not be myself when I reach you.

I was freaked. Mom was freaked. She took the morning off and had the locks changed, even though she said that "M" could be anyone, that this had nothing to do with our missing key, and that the note could have been stuck in that book by anyone, years ago probably, and we'd never know why.

"Isn't it weird, though?" I said. "Our key was just stolen on Friday, and now on Monday we find a note asking where our key is?"

"It *is* weird," Mom said. She put her hands on her hips. "But if you think about it, one thing really can't have anything to do with the other. Someone *with* the key wouldn't have to *ask* where the key is. It makes no sense."

She was right, of course. It was backward. But somewhere in my head a tiny bell started ringing. I didn't even notice it at first.

Things on a Slant

Our second week, Jimmy said we could start serving customers.

"But first you have to learn the V-cut," he told us. "Very important." Except he said "Velly important," stretched his eyelids back with two fingers, and bowed down low—it was the classic fake-Chinese act. I had never seen a grown-up do it before. If Mom had been there, she would have whacked him on the head with a plastic tray.

"The V-what?" Colin said.

The V-cut was Jimmy's special way of cutting the sandwich rolls. "Always a forty-five-degree angle," he said. He was very serious about it, sawing down one side of the roll and then carefully sliding the knife out and inserting it in the other side.

The top of the bread was supposed to lift off in a perfect "V," which was why Jimmy called it a V-cut. He gave us each a roll and watched while we tried it. Annemarie's was perfect. Colin's was passable. Mine was a disaster. When I lifted the top off, flaps of bread guts were hanging down, and Jimmy said it looked "unappealing."

"You can use that for your own sandwich," he said, making a face at my shredded roll. "Try again tomorrow."

So Annemarie and Colin got to put on aprons, stand behind the counter, and help customers while I counted the bread order in the back and went to the A&P for napkins. Annemarie said later that Jimmy should talk, that *he* looked "unappealing" in his stretched-out white T-shirt with yellow underarm stains. That made me feel a little better, but not much.

As soon as Colin got his apron on, Jimmy started calling him "lady"—"Hey, lady, get some more mayo on there." "Hey, lady, pass me those trays." Colin just laughed, which is how Colin is.

Every day that week, I cut my roll as soon as I got to the store, and every day Jimmy shook his head no. Colin and Annemarie worked together behind the counter—Jimmy had started calling them the counter couple and making disgusting kissing noises at them when he walked by, which made Annemarie turn red, while Colin just smiled like a goofball.

Jimmy said that while I practiced my V-cut I could be in charge of hot chocolate. He used those Swiss Miss instant hot chocolate packets where you just add water. But no one ever ordered it. And I don't think he really even looked at my rolls after the first couple of days. Anyway, they were only getting worse.

White Things

The first time I brought Annemarie home to our apartment after school, I wished for two things. First, I wished that the boys wouldn't be in front of the garage. They'd just recently started saying things to me, different things, some of which included the words "sweet" and "baby." Mom said this happened to girls after a certain age, and that what the boys wanted was a reaction, any kind of reaction.

"Don't laugh, don't call them jerks, don't take off running," she said. "Do nothing. Act as if they're invisible."

My second wish was that the laughing man would be gone, or asleep, or at least distracted by someone or something else when we walked by.

We got to Broadway. "Want to stop for a soda?" I said.

Annemarie shrugged. "No thanks."

We started toward Amsterdam. I tried to follow Annemarie's conversation but mostly just squinted to see down the block. By some miracle, the boys weren't out in front of the garage. I offered up a silent thank you to the universe. And then we started across the street to my corner.

"Angel!" the laughing man called out. He was looking right at Annemarie, and I couldn't help thinking that, depending on your idea of heaven, Annemarie might appear to be something like an angel. Her coat was pure white and went all the way down to her toes, even though it was only the middle of November and really not all that cold. How her dad kept that coat so clean is still a mystery to me.

"Angel!"

I laughed. I was trying to show Annemarie how absolutely downright *funny* it was to have a weird homeless guy here on my corner. My very own weird homeless guy!

"Ha. 'Angel,' " I said. "That's a new one."

"Angel!" he called out again. And now he was *pointing* at her.

"Is he pointing at me?" Annemarie asked, slowing down.

"No," I said, steering her as far from the laughing man as I could without pushing her into crosstown traffic.

Upstairs, a weird thing happened. After living there almost every day of my life, I saw our apartment as if it were the first time. I noticed all sorts of things that were usually invisible to me: the stuffing coming out of the sofa in two places, the burns from Mr. Nunzi's cigarettes, the big flakes of paint hanging off the ceiling, and the black spot next to the radiator where dripping water had stained the wood floor.

"Excuse me," I said. "I'll be right back."

In the bathroom, I stared at the white tile hexagons on the floor and saw nothing but the crud in between them. I hid Mom's twenty-year-old jar of Vaseline in the medicine cabinet that's been painted so many times it won't close anymore.

"I like your room," Annemarie called to me when I came out of the bathroom. I turned slowly and looked into my room, wondering what horror I would see in it. But it actually looked okay: no curtains or carpeting, but normal stuff, a normal room with a friend sitting on the bed, which had just one pillow. I stepped in and closed the door behind me.

When Mom got home, we walked Annemarie back to her building. Luckily, the laughing man was under his mailbox by that time. I wanted Mom to be surprised when Annemarie's doorman called me Miss Miranda, but she just smiled at him.

I could tell that Annemarie's dad was charmed by Mom—people always like her. He offered us some kind of powdered-sugar dough balls he had in the kitchen, and Mom ate two of them while I said no thank you, that I hadn't had my dinner yet, which made Mom laugh and cough up powdered sugar, which made Annemarie's dad laugh. I looked at the sugar on the front of her T-shirt and thought that if she had the slightest idea what she looked like, she wouldn't be laughing at all.

The Second Note

The sandwich rolls are delivered to Jimmy's store early in the morning, before he gets there. I still see the tall paper bag leaning against his locked door on my way to school every day. I haven't put one foot inside Jimmy's place since December, but I look for that bag out of habit, and when I see it, I always think I can smell the bread inside, which I know is just a memory.

Last November, I counted Jimmy's bread delivery at lunch every day, pulling the rolls out by twos and dropping them into the previous day's empty bag as I went. I remember finding your second note about halfway down, on a Monday.

Same weird tiny handwriting, same crispy paper. But this one started with my name.

> Miranda:
>   Your letter must tell a story—a true story. You cannot begin now, as most of it has not yet taken place. And even afterward, there is no hurry. But do not wait so long

that your memory fades. I require as much
detail as you can provide. The trip is a
difficult one, and I must ask my favors while
my mind is sound.

A postscript: I know you have shared my
first note. I ask you not to share the others.
Please. I do not ask this for myself.

I read the note over and over. But I have to tell you
that I had no idea what any of it meant, until later.
And I have to tell you something else, too: I was
scared. You scared the hell out of me.

"You counting those rolls or memorizing them?"
Jimmy was behind the counter, running a hunk of
ham back and forth in the electric slicer really fast, the
way he liked to.

I stuffed the note in my pocket and started counting bread again, but I'd lost my place and I had to start
all over.

A few minutes later, a delivery truck pulled up in
front of the store and Jimmy went out to talk to the
driver.

"Hey," Colin said as soon as the door had closed
behind Jimmy, "let's find out what's in the Fred Flintstone bank."

"No way," Annemarie said. "You're crazy."

"You're the lookout," I told her, following Colin
into the back room. He had the bank in his hands already. He shook it, but it made almost no noise.

"You *guys*," Annemarie said. *"Don't."*

"We're just looking at it!" I called back. "Hurry," I said to Colin. He was trying to get the rubber stopper out of the bottom of the bank.

"Let me try," I whispered.

"No," he said, "I've got it." And the stopper was in his hand.

We bumped foreheads trying to see into the hole at the same time, and then left our heads pressed together, which was something I hadn't expected to do. I couldn't quite see Colin's face from this perspective, but I felt him smile.

"Cool," he said. "It's full of two-dollar bills!"

He was right. The bank was practically stuffed with two-dollar bills, folded into little triangle shapes, with the "2's" showing on the sides.

"You guys, he's *coming*." Annemarie sounded panicked. We pulled our heads apart and Colin shoved the rubber stopper back in. I was out front by the time Jimmy held the door open for the delivery guy, who had a stack of sodas loaded onto a hand truck.

"Hey, lady!" Jimmy called. "I need you. This is man's work."

"Sorry." Colin came strolling out of the back in his apron. "Bathroom break."

Annemarie smiled at me while Colin and Jimmy were busy loading the soda into the big refrigerated case by the door.

"You're nuts," she said. "You know that, right?"

I could still feel the spot where Colin's head had

pressed up against mine. "I know. It was kind of stupid."

We walked back to school with Colin between us. He was zigzagging and bumping his shoulders against ours, saying, "Boing! Five points. Boing! Ten points," while we both laughed like idiots.

Things You Push Away

"Ready?" Richard asks Mom. We are practicing even more now. He sits in a chair opposite her. I'm the timekeeper. Mom closes her eyes, and I know that she is lifting a corner of her veil. She nods, and we begin.

Mom says each of us has a veil between ourselves and the rest of the world, like a bride wears on her wedding day, except this kind of veil is invisible. We walk around happily with these invisible veils hanging down over our faces. The world is kind of blurry, and we like it that way.

But sometimes our veils are pushed away for a few moments, like there's a wind blowing it from our faces. And when the veil lifts, we can see the world as it really is, just for those few seconds before it settles down again. We see all the beauty, and cruelty, and sadness, and love. But mostly we are happy not to. Some people learn to lift the veil themselves. Then they don't have to depend on the wind anymore.

She doesn't mean that it's a real veil. And it isn't about magic, or some idea that maybe God is looking right at you, or an angel is sitting next to you, or anything like that. Mom doesn't think in those ways. It's just her way of saying that most of the time, people get distracted by little stuff and ignore the big stuff.

To play in the Winner's Circle, Mom has to get herself in a certain frame of mind. She says it's sort of like lifting one little corner of her veil, enough to see more than usual but not so much that she gets totally distracted by life, death, and the beauty of it all. She has to open her mind, she says, so that when the clues start coming, she can see the thread that joins them. Of course, if her celebrity is as dumb as a bag of hair, it's hopeless.

I've thought a lot about those veils. I wonder if, every once in a while, someone is born without one. Someone who sees the big stuff all the time. Like maybe you.

Things You Count

Right before Thanksgiving, Colin and Annemarie were behind the counter weighing a slimy heap of sliced turkey into quarter-pound piles separated by pieces of waxed paper. Jimmy said they should do a whole week's worth.

"Won't it go bad?" Annemarie asked.

"Nah. Stuff's full of preservatives."

Colin licked his lips and said, "Yum, yum. Chemical turkey."

"Shut it," Jimmy said.

For once, I was happy to be counting the rolls.

Now that he had us, Jimmy seemed to have nothing to do. He sat on one of the stools bolted to the floor in front of the big front window and watched me with his arms crossed over his chest, his hands tucked under his yellow-stained armpits. He had already rejected my V-cut for the day—it was waiting for me on a tray behind Annemarie, getting dry as usual. Luckily, Jimmy didn't limit our use of mayonnaise.

"Lookie," Jimmy said, pointing his chin toward the window. "There goes one of your little friends."

On the other side of the street, Julia was walking alone, wearing her orange suede knapsack and an orange suede headband that matched. Matching suede knapsacks and headbands were probably all the rage in Switzerland, I thought.

"You mean Swiss Miss?" I grabbed two rolls and dropped them into the bag at my feet. "She's not my friend. Not even close."

He smiled slowly. "Swiss Miss. That's a good one." He stared outside for another minute and then stood up. "You're funny, you know that?"

I shrugged, still counting, but happy. A compliment from Jimmy was a rare thing. When I finished, I folded the top of the bag and lugged it to its spot behind the counter. Jimmy had disappeared into the back. Annemarie was giggling at something Colin had said.

Ever since our foreheads had touched, looking at Colin made me feel strange. But good-strange, not creepy-strange.

"Eighty!" I called out to Jimmy. Right on the nose.

"Better luck next time!" he yelled back.

Colin looked at me and grinned, causing my stomach to sort of float inside my body. "He's dying for the bread order to come up short, you know. You should throw a roll in the trash one day, just to make him happy."

"Don't listen to him, Miranda," Annemarie said. "He's just trying to get you in trouble again."

But while she was talking to me, she was looking at Colin, and her expression was funny, as if her stomach might be floating too.

Messy Things

Annemarie and I stopped in the fourth-floor bathroom before going back to class after lunch. She said she wanted to wash her hands again after all that turkey.

"Today was fun," she said, looking at herself in the mirror and combing her hair with her fingers. "I wish we got more than forty minutes for lunch."

"I hate counting bread," I said. "It's boring."

She laughed. "At least your hands don't smell like chemical turkey."

At least you get to goof around behind the counter with Colin, I thought. I'm always running to the store, cleaning up some gunk, or stuck talking to Mr. Yellow Stains.

"Let's go," I said. "I'm starving."

Julia was standing right outside our classroom, almost as if she was waiting for us.

"Oh, no!" She sighed deeply and pointed at Annemarie's arm. "Oh, Annemarie, your turquoise sweater. It's your favorite. Poor you!"

And Mom thought *I* was dramatic.

Annemarie looked down at the hem of her sweater, which had some mustard on it. I had no idea it was her favorite.

"It'll come out," Annemarie said. "My dad will get it out."

Julia leaned against the wall and adjusted her headband. "What I don't understand is why you're working at all. It's not like you need the money." Here she stopped to glance at me. "And no offense, but that place is kind of disgusting. I saw a roach there once."

"I like it there," Annemarie said. "It's actually pretty fun."

"That guy who works there is gross."

"He's not gross!" I said. "And he doesn't"—I made air quotes—"'work there.' He owns the store."

"We don't get paid," Annemarie said softly. "It's just the sandwiches."

"And sodas," I said, waving my Sprite.

"Right," Julia said, talking just to Annemarie, as if I didn't exist. "Like you're supposed to be eating sandwiches and drinking soda."

Annemarie's face folded up a little. "It's fine."

"Fine," Julia said. "Forget it."

Mr. Tompkin came to the door. "Why aren't you three inside? Silent reading period started five minutes ago."

As we walked in behind Julia, I whispered to Annemarie, "No wonder you don't want to be friends with her anymore. She's *so* rude to you."

For a second Annemarie didn't say anything. Then

she mumbled, "Yeah, sometimes," and we separated to go to our desks.

Mr. Tompkin had left a book on my desk. He was always trying to get me to read something new. This one had a picture of a spunky-looking girl on the cover, and some buildings behind her. I pushed the spunky girl aside, pulled *my* book out of my desk, and opened it randomly to see where I would land.

Meg was on the planet Camazotz where all these little boys are in front of their matching houses, bouncing their matching balls. All the balls hit the ground at exactly the same moment, every time. Then all the boys turn at the same second and go back into their identical houses. Except for this one boy. He's outside all alone, and his ball rolls into the street, and then his mother comes out looking all nervous and carries him into the house.

I was thinking about how much Mr. Tompkin would hate the idea of a place where all the houses look exactly the same when something stung me hard behind the ear. I jerked my head up and saw Julia laughing silently over her book. I looked down on the floor and saw the rubber band she had shot at me. At my head.

I'd thought we were just irritating each other, but I was wrong. This was war.

Invisible Things

The next time I saw Marcus, I was absolutely sure he would remember me. I was in the main office, because Mr. Tompkin had sent me down to pick up some mimeographs.

"Why you kids need diagrams of the water system is beyond me," Wheelie said as she handed them to me from her chair.

"They're for Main Street," I told her. "We're trying to make working hydrants."

"Well, that may be the silliest thing I've ever heard," she said, waving me away.

I love the smell of new copies. Mom says I have an attraction to dangerous smells, her main example being the fact that I love to stand in a warm cloud of dry-cleaner exhaust and take deep breaths. There is something very food-but-not-food about the smell of dry-cleaner exhaust. She always pulls me away and says that she's sure in ten years we'll find out that it causes horrible diseases.

I was walking back toward the stairs, quietly

inhaling the smell of the thirty-two freshly copied diagrams of the New York City water system, when Marcus came out of the stairwell reading a book.

"Hey," I said, but he walked right by me, past the main office, and around the corner to where the dentist's office is.

Back in class, I passed out the diagrams like Mr. Tompkin asked me to. I accidentally ripped Julia's before I gave it to her, and accidentally crumpled it a little too. Alice Evans was squirming in her chair like she was doing a hula dance. I rolled my eyes. No wonder she was the only sixth grader who had to bring an extra set of clothes to school.

Things You Hold On To

According to Jimmy, there's a two-dollar bill in circulation for every twelve one-dollar bills.

"But people hold on to them," he said while I was putting on my jacket to go to the store. The lightbulb over the sink in the back room had burned out, and Jimmy didn't have any extras. "People think two-dollar bills are special. That's why you don't see them around much."

Yeah, I thought. People like you! But I kept my face blank, because I wasn't supposed to know what was in his Fred Flintstone bank.

"They hate 'em over at the A&P, though. No space in a cash register for a two-dollar bill. They gotta pull out the tray and store them underneath. And they always forget they're in there. That's why you have to ask for them."

"Okay," I said. "I'll ask."

Annemarie was behind the counter with her apron on, looking happy. Some kids from school had come in—paying customers—and she was writing their names in mayonnaise on their sandwiches before pressing her perfect V-tops down onto them. Colin was next to her, doing the same. Annemarie gestured me over. I noticed that she was either very warm or she was wearing makeup.

"I'm going to ask Jimmy if we can have meatballs for lunch," she whispered. "Since it's Thanksgiving tomorrow."

"Great," I said, even though I didn't find those meatballs any more appealing than my usual cheese sandwich. They just sat there in the pot, day after day. "I'll be back in a minute," I told her. "If anyone orders hot chocolate, tell them to wait for me."

There were no two-dollar bills at the A&P, and when I got back to Jimmy's with the lightbulbs, the kids were gone and Julia herself was standing in front of the sandwich counter. Annemarie and Colin had started making their lunches already. Jimmy had said no, I guessed, to the meatballs, because they were picking through the cheese.

Julia, who was pretending I hadn't just walked in, seemed to be in the middle of a long speech about how American cheese wasn't even real cheese, strictly speaking. I saw her long fingers gesturing toward the not-cheese, and I knew instantly that her V-cut would be flawless, that by Monday she would be behind that counter with Annemarie and Colin, and that her apron, the same kind that looked gray and baggy on everyone else, would somehow be perfect on her. She would have a way of tucking it up to fit, some trick a waiter in Paris had taught her.

Then Jimmy came out from the back room holding a stack of dripping plastic trays. "You." He pointed at Julia with an armful of trays. "Out. I already told you once."

Julia snatched her hand back from the setup tray. Annemarie flushed. "We're just talking," Annemarie said. "There's no customers here now."

"Actually, *I'm* a customer," Julia said, crossing her arms over her chest. "I came to buy a sandwich. I have money." She stuck out one pretty boot so that the green leather tip pointed at the ceiling.

"Out," Jimmy said, practically growling. "Now."

After she left, I pretended along with Annemarie that Jimmy was a little bit crazy, but as we walked back to school with our cheese-and-lettuce sandwiches, I carried a new warm feeling inside. Jimmy could be a grouch, but he saw right through Julia, just like I did.

Salty Things

On the Friday after Thanksgiving there was no school, but Mom still had to go to work. I'd been trying hard not to think about them, but I spent a good chunk of that morning worrying about your notes. I held one in each hand and read them over and over. The part about writing a letter wasn't too scary. The scary parts were "I'm coming to save your friend's life" and "Oh, by the way, where do you keep your keys?" and "P.S. Don't ever tell anyone about any of this." Seeing my name written out on the second note was also pretty creepy, because I was still trying to pretend the notes weren't really meant for me. And also where you wrote "I won't be myself when I reach you." I didn't like that part at all.

Come to think of it, there were a lot of scary parts.

After a long time, I put the notes away and turned on the television. I had been watching TV for two hours when I heard Louisa's regular knock.

"Potato-chip drop," she said when I opened the door. She was in her uniform, holding up a plastic bag.

Louisa is always bringing Mom food from the

nursing home where she works. She doesn't steal—it's leftovers from lunch, mostly little bags of potato chips or animal cookies. The health department says that once something has been served on a tray, it has to be thrown away even if no one touched it. So Louisa takes all the little bags home and gives them to Mom, who brings them to the pregnant-jailbird "parenting group" she runs downtown.

Once a month, Mom takes the subway down to this actual jail and talks to criminal pregnant women about what to expect after they have their babies. They all think she's some kind of saint for bringing them potato chips and animal cookies. Mom says that jail is a hard place, and that it can make people hard, too.

"It changes them," she told me once. "Jail stops them from becoming who they might grow to be."

"Isn't that the whole idea?" I asked. "It's supposed to stop them from being criminals!"

She shook her head. "That's not what I mean. A lot of people make bad mistakes. But being in jail can make them feel like a mistake is all they are. Like they aren't even people anymore."

Her bringing the chips and cookies is supposed to help somehow. It's not really the cookies, she says. It's the fact that someone brings them.

I took the plastic bag from Louisa.

She smiled at me. "You know what? You're getting tall."

I leaned against the doorway. "You think?"

She nodded. "I miss you, Miranda." It was the first time either of us had said anything about the fact that I was never at her apartment anymore.

"Yeah."

Her saying she missed me made me feel sort of hopeless for some reason. When she left, I lay on the couch with the TV off and my eyes closed, and I listened for Sal's basketball. Hearing it made me feel better, for once. That sound was like the last thread connecting us.

Mom didn't talk much at dinner that night. She was still in her work clothes, a denim skirt and a T-shirt with a picture of a coffee cup on it and the words *Get Your Own* underneath. Richard had brought strawberries over for dessert.

"Darn it." Mom threw down a strawberry. "SSO's again."

"I bet the grapes are delicious." I gave her a fake smile.

"Don't start, Miranda. I had a lousy day."

"You did?" Richard's eyebrows went up. "I didn't know that."

"How would you know?" Mom asked. "You were in court all day. It isn't much to you if the copier breaks, is it? Did anyone ask *you* to type three copies of a sixteen-page document?"

Richard shrugged. "But you're done now. It's over. Why let it wreck your whole evening?"

"Oh, stuff it, Mr. Perfect!" Mom stomped off to her

bedroom without even giving him a chance to tap his right knee.

Richard looked at me. "What did the zero say to the eight?"

I rolled my eyes. "Nice belt." He'd been telling me that one for at least a year.

Later, Mom stacked the dishes in the sink, turned the faucet on, and went to change her clothes. I stood there and watched as the greasy saucepan overflowed onto the plates underneath. The oily water reflected the light and made the whole thing look like a sparkly fountain. Sometimes I can stare at something like that for a long time.

Mom came back wearing sweatpants and started washing the dishes. I opened my math workbook at the kitchen table. A minute later, Richard came in and said, "Didn't I leave that extra pair of work shoes here a few months ago? I know they were in the closet, but I can't find them anywhere."

Mom's head snapped up. "I knew it. I just knew it." We had been robbed after all.

Things You Pretend

The Monday after Thanksgiving we were stuck in the school cafeteria for lunch. The naked guy was back, running down Broadway, and they wouldn't let any kids out of the building.

"Kind of cold out to be running around in your birthday suit!" Colin called over to us on his way to a table of boys. Annemarie giggled. I could see Sal over there. He'd glanced toward us once, but acted like he didn't see me.

I watched the boys for a few seconds, all of them trying to talk louder than the other ones. Sal was doing it, too—every once in a while I could hear his voice on top, and it reminded me of this game we used to play on the crosstown bus on our way to the city pool. Sal would be holding on to the silver bus pole, and I would grab the pole right above his hand. Then he'd move his hand so it was right above mine, and I'd put mine on top of his, until we were on our tiptoes, holding on to the pole near the very top, and usually some grown-up would say to stop fooling around, couldn't we see the bus was crowded and one of us was going to fall and knock somebody over.

Annemarie picked at her food. The worst part of being stuck inside for lunch was that we had to get school lunch, which was gross.

"I wonder if Jimmy will count the bread order himself," I said. "I bet he won't. I think he just likes to make me do it."

She nodded. "To give you something to do."

"Gee, thanks." I threw my milk straw at her.

"Hey! I didn't mean—"

"Sure you didn't!"

Then her smile faded. She was still looking at me, but something had changed, like a switch had been flicked inside her. Like she was still there but was doing something else in her head.

"Annemarie?"

"Don't." Julia was standing behind me with a carton of milk in her hand. Before I could say anything, she slid onto the bench next to me, still looking right at Annemarie. "She'll be fine in a minute."

"What's wrong with her?"

"Just wait." Julia hadn't even glanced at me. Her eyes never left Annemarie's face.

Annemarie moved her head a little. She put her arm down on the table, blinked, and said, "What?" as if she had maybe missed something I'd just said.

"Are you okay?" I asked.

Julia hit my knee with hers under the table. "Don't ask her questions," she hissed.

Annemarie noticed her just then. "Hi, Julia," she said, and a smile came over her face.

Julia smiled back. "Hi." Then she turned to me. "So, Miranda, how's the playground going? For Main Street, I mean."

She wanted to talk about Main Street? Now?

Her eyes held mine. "I heard your proposal was approved. Congratulations."

Congratulations? "Uh, thanks."

"Will there be swings? How are you going to make them?"

It was dawning on me that Julia was showing me something, teaching me how to help Annemarie.

"Paper clips," I told Julia. "I'm using paper clips to make the chains for the swings, and I'm going to cut pieces of rubber tire for the seats."

Julia was nodding. "That sounds great," she said. I could almost imagine us being friends, having this conversation for real.

"What else?" she asked.

"What?"

She looked annoyed. I wasn't catching on fast enough. "For the playground. What else?"

"Oh—well, seesaws. Definitely seesaws."

Then Annemarie spoke. "You know, balsa wood would be perfect for the seesaws—it's really easy to cut. I think my dad might even have some."

"Really?" I said. "That would be great. We could paint them orange, just like the ones in Riverside Park."

"Yes!" Annemarie said. "We can start them at my

house—maybe even today if you want." She looked at Julia. "Want to come? And start Miranda's seesaws?"

Before Julia could answer, I said "There's no rush. I just got the plans approved. We can start next week. Anyway, Annemarie, you were coming to my house today, remember?"

I felt Julia pulling away. "See you guys," she said, and stood up.

"Bye!" I said.

Annemarie looked up at her. "Bye, Julia."

A few minutes later, the PA system crackled to life and Annemarie was called to the nurse's office.

Annemarie shrugged, smiled, and walked away, saying, "See you in a minute."

But she didn't come back.

Things That Crack

Outside our classroom, Julia waited for me with her hands on her hips. "God, you're an idiot. You're an idiot, you know that?"

"*I'm* an idiot?"

"She's been eating all that bread at that stupid job you got her. She's not supposed to eat any of that stuff. Idiot."

"I didn't get her the stupid . . . I don't even know what you're talking about!"

"It's her epilepsy, idiot. You total idiot. Her dad has her on this special diet. He makes her special food. She's not supposed to eat bread, or drink soda."

"She's not?"

"No, she's not. Idiot. And by the way, what's your problem with me, anyway? I'd really like to know."

"What?"

"Your problem. With me. What is it?"

"Besides the fact that you've called me an idiot six times in the last minute? Besides the fact that you shot a rubber band at my *head*?"

She waved all that away as if I had mentioned some

silly detail. "I'm talking about way before that. You've hated me forever. You've been giving me dirty looks since like third grade! Are you going to pretend you haven't?"

I stared at her. Some feeling had started in my stomach and was traveling up to my face, and I knew that when it got there I would turn bright red and hear the ocean, which is what happens when I get put on the spot. If I don't cry, I turn red and hear the ocean. It's a lose-lose situation.

"What are you talking about?" I said.

"I have no idea," she said. "I really don't. But a person knows when someone hates her—at least, I do!" She flung her arm down and her little silver watch flew off her wrist and hit the floor with a crack. A very sharp, final-sounding sort of crack.

Her precious watch. I'm not proud of this now, but that sound, which echoed in the tiled hallway, made me really happy. I sucked my bottom lip so that I wouldn't smile.

Julia bent down to pick up the watch. I thought she would start to screech, but she just flipped it over in her hand and looked at it. A web of tiny cracks covered the face like a cobweb.

"Oh, great." She puffed out her cheeks and exhaled slowly. "This whole day just stinks," she said, and she walked away.

On the way home I found myself walking half a block behind Sal again. I'd learned not to run and catch up to him—he would only look at his sneakers and not talk.

So I watched him bobbing along in his navy blue knit hat, his head going from side to side a little, like it always does when he walks. I think he thought that hat looked tough the way he had it pulled down to his eyebrows.

Then Marcus came out of his dented front door next to the garage, wearing that green army coat he always wore. He started walking down the block—toward Sal.

Even half a block behind him, I could see Sal's body hunch and slow down. I knew what he was doing. He was looking for a way out. Should he pretend he needed to cross the street all of a sudden? That he had just remembered something he needed to buy at Belle's? But it was a little late for that—Marcus was almost in front of him.

I could have called out to Sal at that moment. It would have been easy. He would have had an excuse to turn around and start walking away from Marcus. And then Marcus might have stopped to talk to me for a minute, and Sal would have seen that it was all okay. He could have dropped his fear of Marcus right then and there. I've thought about this a lot, because I realize it would have changed everything that happened later.

Instead I watched. And what Sal did was squat down and pretend to tie his shoe. It was a plea for mercy. Dropping to tie your shoe was an I-can't-fight, I-can't-run, I-bow-down-before-you sort of a move. Plus, just in case some hitting did occur, it protected important body parts. I kept walking while Sal crouched there on the sidewalk and Marcus walked right by without even noticing him. And then Marcus walked right by me.

Things Left Behind

"Guess what?" Annemarie said when I called her at home that night to see if she was okay. "Someone left a rose on our doormat."

"For you?"

"I don't know . . . maybe." Of course it was for her. Who else would it be for?

"Was there anything with it? A card?"

"No. Just the rose." Her voice sounded all thin and excited. "Weird, huh? I wonder—"

"Hey, can I ask you something? Are you not supposed to eat bread?"

She was quiet.

"It's not a big deal, just that Julia said—"

"No," she interrupted. "It *is* sort of a big deal. I should have told you. I have epilepsy—"

"Oh."

"—and I'm not supposed to eat bread or starches. It's this crazy diet my dad read about, but it actually works. I'm usually fine. People don't even really know I have it, because for years I've hardly had any seizures at all."

"Is that what happened today?

"Yeah. I sort of took a break from my diet. It's been nice, working at Jimmy's with you guys, eating whatever I want and not having anyone look at me funny or lecture me."

Someone had lectured her, though. Julia had.

"You can still work at Jimmy's," I said. "Just don't eat his crummy food."

She laughed. "I know. Actually, my dad makes me a lunch every day. I've been throwing it in the garbage on the way to school. He's pretty mad."

That was hard to imagine.

"Anyway, my mother found this rose on our door-mat when she got home from work. It's like this really perfect-looking rose. Weird, huh?"

I let her talk about it a little more, about who might have left it, and why. I knew she wanted me to say that Colin probably did it, but I just couldn't make myself say the words.

The Third Note

The next morning was the first really cold day of December.

"You need the jacket with the hood," Mom rasped from her bed. Her voice never sounded normal until after coffee. "Look in the front closet." She seemed to think that it was really helpful to lie in bed, listening to the radio and calling out weather reports. I couldn't help thinking about how, in my book, Meg's mother had French toast waiting for Meg in the morning. She was a single mom too, with Meg's dad being held prisoner halfway across the universe.

I found the coat, still streaked with gray from last year's dirty snow, and put it on. A little stiff, but it seemed to fit okay.

"Where are my gloves?" I called.

"No idea. Sorry."

"Can I take some money?"

"Coat pocket."

I felt around in her coat and found a five-dollar bill and three singles in one pocket and her striped scarf rolled up in the other. I grabbed the singles and the scarf.

"Bye!"

The laughing man was still asleep with his head under the mailbox. He had found some cardboard to put underneath him. Still, he must have been freezing. Some mornings, I'd seen kids banging on the mailbox and yelling, "Wake up, Kicker!" I hoped no one would do that today.

I watched my breath billowing in front of me and racewalked toward school. The sun was out but had no warmth yet. I shoved my hands in my pockets and felt a bunch of old tissues. Yuck. And the three dollars. And something else, a little piece of paper, folded in half.

I pulled it out.

I recognized your tiny handwriting right away, all wobbly and with those weird loops you put on top of your "t's" and "l's."

> You will want proof.
> 3 p.m. today: Colin's knapsack.
> Christmas Day: Tesser well.
> April 27th: Studio TV-15.
> P.S. Yawns do serve a purpose. They
> cool the brain by bringing air high into the
> nasal passage, which has the effect of
> increasing alertness.

The note was on the same dried-up paper as the first two.

3 p.m. today: Colin's knapsack. I had absolutely no idea what that could mean, or how you knew Colin.

Christmas Day: Tesser well. This one had something to do with my book. To tesser meant to travel, through space or time or both. It was how Meg got to Camazotz, the planet where her father was held prisoner. But it had nothing to do with Christmas, as far as I knew.

April 27th: Studio TV-15. April 27 was Richard's birthday. But of course back in December I had never heard of Studio TV-15, since Mom didn't get her postcard from *The $20,000 Pyramid* until a couple of weeks ago.

I think it was the "P.S." that freaked me out most. I thought of the day Sal got punched, when I had carried my *Mysteries of Science* poster home.

I read the note over and over, until my hands were frozen and I was forced to put them back in my pockets. It made no sense. The only thing it really helped me understand was that you were watching me. And I had no idea who you were. Or what you wanted.

I was almost to the garage when Marcus came out of his door right in front of me. He had on his regular green army jacket, but he was wearing gloves and had a hat pulled down over his ears. I expected him to ignore me like he always did, but instead he waved and started walking along next to me.

Things That Make No Sense

Marcus and I got to Broadway without saying anything. I was thinking.

"I thought of a question for you," I said finally.

"Okay."

"Let's say I build a time machine." I waited to see if he would laugh at this, but he just nodded and looked thoughtful. "And let's say I decide I want to go back to last Wednesday. Let's say I want to go to the movies while the other me is still in school."

"Okay."

I exhaled a big white cloud. "I won't *get* to last Wednesday until after I leave, right? I mean, I won't know if I'm really going to get there until I actually *get* there."

"Right. In *your* experience, you won't know if you're going to get there until after you leave. I mean, unless you remember seeing yourself, on the street or something. Or we could ask the ticket guy at the theater." He was serious.

"What?"

"At the movie theater. Which one are you planning to go to? Because we could ask the ticket guy if you were there. Then we'll know whether or not you're going to get there."

"But I haven't left yet! I haven't even built the time machine."

"So? It doesn't matter when you *leave*. It's just whether or not you *get there* that matters. Wait, I take that back. It does matter when you leave. Because if you don't leave for fifty years, even if you *were* there, the ticket guy probably won't recognize you."

"What are you talking about?"

"Well, let's say you finish your time machine in fifty years. You'd be—"

"Sixty-two," I said. We were across the street from school, waiting for the green light. I could see kids coming from every direction, all bundled up in hats and scarves.

"Okay, so let's say you're sixty-two, and you climb into your machine and go back to last Wednesday, December whatever, 1978. You go to the movie theater. The ticket guy would see a sixty-two-year-old woman, right?"

"Right," I said. So far everything made sense.

"So if we went over to the theater today and asked him whether he saw you there last Wednesday, he'd say no. Because his common sense would tell him that you can't be that sixty-two-year-old woman, and she can't be you. Get it?"

I shook my head. "If we asked *today,* he couldn't have seen me anyway. I wouldn't have been there yet. Because I haven't *gone back* yet."

"*Duh,*" said a voice behind us. "It's really not all that complicated."

I whirled around and saw Julia in a long coat. She was standing right behind us waiting for the light.

Marcus ignored her and looked at me. "Are you still worrying about that book? About the kids, and seeing themselves land in the broccoli?"

I said nothing. I wasn't going to have Julia hear any more of this conversation.

"Think of it like this," Marcus said, oblivious to the look she was giving us. "Time isn't a line stretching out in front of us, going in one direction. It's—well, time is just a construct, actually—"

"Look," Julia said, cutting him off. "If you really need to know what he means, *I'll* explain it to you."

This should be good, I thought. Julia is going to explain the nature of time.

I turned around and looked at her. "Fine. Go ahead."

She pulled off one of her gloves—they were these beautiful, fuzzy, pale yellow gloves—and she yanked a ring from her finger. "I think of it like this," she said, holding up the ring. It was gold, studded all the way around with—

"Are those *diamonds?*" I said.

"Diamond chips." She shrugged. "Look. It's like every moment in time is a diamond sitting on this ring. Pretend the ring is really big, with diamonds all around, and each diamond is one moment. Got it?"

Marcus was silent, just looking at her.

I laughed. "Time is a diamond ring!" I said. "That explains everything. Thanks."

"Would you shut up and listen? If you figured out a way to bring yourself to another time, probably through some sort of teleportation—you'd be somehow *re-creating* your atoms, really, not physically moving them, I'm guessing; that would be tricky. . . ."

"Can we not worry about that part right now?" I said. "I'm freezing." We were still standing across the street from school, even though the light had changed once already and then gone back to red.

"Okay. Put it this way—we're kind of jumping from diamond to diamond, like in cartoons where someone is running on a barrel, trying to stay on top. We have to keep moving—there's no choice."

"Now we're in a cartoon, on a barrel?"

She sighed and shook her head. "Okay, forget that. Let's stick with the ring." She held it up again. "Let's say we're here." She put her fingernail on one diamond chip. "And we figure out a way to jump all the way back to here." She pointed to another one, a few chips away. "It wouldn't matter where we came from. If we're on that chip, we're at that moment. It doesn't matter whether we came from the chip behind it, or ten chips ahead of it. If we're there, we're there. Get it?"

"No. I don't get it, because what you're saying makes absolutely no—"

"I do," Marcus said quietly. "I get it. I know what she means."

"*Thank* you!" Julia said. "I'm glad *someone* here has a brain." And she stomped off through the red light while Marcus stared after her.

I turned to him. "So you're saying this diamond *chip* is just sitting there minding its own business, and then suddenly a bunch of kids land in the diamond chip's *broccoli patch*—"

Marcus's face lit up. "Stop—I see your problem! You're thinking that time exists on the diamonds themselves. It doesn't. Each moment—each diamond—is like a snapshot."

"A snapshot of what?"

"Of everything, everywhere! There's no time in a picture, right? It's the *jumping,* from one diamond to the next, that we call time, but like I said, time doesn't really *exist.* Like that girl just said, a diamond is a moment, and all the diamonds on the ring are happening *at the same time.* It's like having a drawer full of pictures."

"On the ring," I said.

"Yes! All the diamonds exist at once!" He looked triumphant. "So if you jump backward, you are at that moment—you are *in that picture*—and you always *were* there, you always *will be* there, even if you don't know it yet."

I didn't understand a word of it. And I couldn't feel my feet. "Forget it," I said. "The whole thing is making me crazy."

He nodded like he felt sorry for me and my stupid

brain. "I think that's probably because of your common sense. You can't accept the idea of arriving before you leave, the idea that every moment is happening at the same time, that it's *us* who are moving—"

Enough was enough. I cut him off. "Why did you hit Sal?" I asked.

"Who?" He looked completely mystified, as if I had just changed the subject from something very normal to something completely insane, instead of the other way around.

"My friend Sal. You punched him in the stomach for no reason. In front of the garage. And then you hit him in the face."

He nodded. "Yes," he said. "That's right. But no—there *was* a reason."

"That's bull. I know he never did a thing to you." I'd started to really shiver, even with my hands stuffed in my pockets and Mom's scarf wrapped around my head.

"I *did* hit him for a reason," he said. "What you're talking about is a justification. I'm not saying it was the right thing to do. I'm just saying I did it for a reason. My own stupid reason."

I stared at him. "So what was the reason?"

He looked down and shrugged. "Same reason I do most things. I wanted to see what would happen."

"What do you mean, 'what would happen'? His nose started bleeding, that's what happened! And he almost threw up."

"Besides that, besides the ordinary things." He

tapped the toe of one shoe on the sidewalk. "It was dumb. Really, really dumb."

"And?"

"And what?"

"And *did* anything happen? Besides the ordinary things?"

He shook his head. "No—not that I could tell."

I was going to tell him that he was wrong, that other things *had* happened, like Sal closing the door in my face that afternoon and never opening it again, but at that moment I noticed the laughing man coming down the block behind us. I'd never seen him near school before. He was bent forward, mumbling and watching his feet, with his eyes on the garbage can right next to Marcus.

The laughing man didn't notice us standing there until he was practically on top of Marcus. When he finally looked up, he cursed, twisted away, and took off in the other direction, sprinting like he was running a race.

We watched him rush all the way back to Broadway and disappear around the corner.

"That was weird," I said.

"Yeah," Marcus agreed. "And it's the second time it's happened."

The First Proof

"What did I tell you?" Jimmy said at lunch that same day, happily slapping the counter with both hands. "They never think you'll actually count the bread. Never in a million years would they think you'd count!" The bread order had come up two rolls short. I'd counted it twice to make sure.

Jimmy swaggered over to the phone with a huge smile on his face.

"You just made his day," Colin whispered. "Maybe his whole week." He was folding slices of ham and laying them out neatly on little squares of waxed paper.

I watched Colin's fingers as they picked up each piece of ham—he didn't just smack them in half like I saw Jimmy do. Colin sort of bent each slice into a pretty fan shape. Once I started watching, I couldn't stop. It was hypnotizing, somehow.

"I talked to Annemarie last night," I said. "I think she's coming back to school tomorrow."

Colin nodded. "Good." It was hard to imagine him sneaking around and leaving a rose on anyone's doormat, but I guess boys will surprise you sometimes.

"Hey," he said suddenly, "you know what? I'm sick of cheese-and-lettuce sandwiches." He glanced guiltily at Jimmy, who was still on the phone talking about his missing rolls. "Want to go get a slice of pizza?"

We acted like everything was normal, making our sandwiches and wrapping them up like we planned to eat them at school. And then we ran to the pizza place down the block. It was crazy, but we felt like we were doing something wrong. We rushed back to school stuffing pizza into our mouths and crouching down low when we passed Jimmy's window so he couldn't see us. Somehow we became so completely hysterical that we were still having what Mom calls fits of helpless laughter when we got to school.

We must have sort of burst into the classroom, because everyone looked up from their silent reading to stare at us. Julia rolled her eyes.

"You're late again," Mr. Tompkin said. And then the whole feeling dissolved and we went to find our books.

I sat with my book open on my desk, thinking about the note in my coat pocket: *3 p.m. today: Colin's knapsack. Your first "proof."* I had to get a look inside Colin's bag, to find whatever would—or wouldn't—be waiting for me.

At three on the dot, I went to the coat closet and grabbed my knapsack to go home. Colin's was just a few hooks away. I could hear him talking to Jay Stringer in the back of the room, near Main Street.

Julia was standing with them, trying again to convince Jay about her stupid tinfoil UFO and how it was going to fly up and down the street on a stupid invisible wire. She still hadn't gotten her project approved.

I reached over and unzipped Colin's bag. There was his denim-covered binder stuffed with falling-out papers, a paperback, and the cheese sandwich he hadn't eaten at lunch, soaking through its paper and smelling like pickles. Nothing unusual.

I felt around the bottom of the bag and touched some keys on a ring, resting in a pile of dirt, or maybe crushed leaves. I tipped the bag toward the light and saw that it wasn't a pile of dirt—it was a pile of crumbs. Bread crumbs.

I patted the back of the bag, felt a lump, reached behind his binder, and pulled out two of Jimmy's rolls. They were flaking all over the place. Colin must have grabbed them straight out of the delivery bag when nobody was looking.

Things You Give Away

I dropped the rolls back into Colin's bag, pulled my coat on, threw my knapsack over one shoulder, and took the stairs two at a time. There was a mob of kids outside like always, pushing and laughing and standing around talking, even though it was still freezing and had started to rain. I took a minute to look for Sal, like I always do. No sign of him. I wound Mom's scarf around my ears, turned north, and started walking up the hill to Annemarie's.

It didn't make sense. Not that Colin had taken the rolls—in fact, that was just the kind of thing I expected from Colin. But my brain was yelling all kinds of other questions at me: How could anyone possibly have *known* that Colin would take the rolls? And when had the note been put in my coat pocket? It didn't occur to me that you could have left it there the same day you put the first note in my library book about the squirrel village. I didn't get that at all, until much later.

And why *me?* I jumped a gutter full of rainwater and took the last steps to Annemarie's building. Why was I the one getting notes? Why did I have to do something about whatever bad thing was going to happen? I didn't even understand what I was supposed to do! Write a letter about something that hadn't happened yet?

"Miranda," my brain said. "Nothing is going to happen. Someone is playing with you." But what if my brain was wrong? What if someone's life really needed saving? What if it wasn't a game?

Annemarie's doorman waved me in. Upstairs, her father answered the door with an unlit cigar in his mouth and asked me whether I wanted some cold noodles with sesame sauce.

"Uh, no thanks."

"Fizzy lemonade, then?" He helped me tug my wet coat off—the lining was all stuck to my sweater.

So I walked into Annemarie's room balancing my lemonade and an ice water for her, along with a dish of almonds that her father had somehow warmed up. Warm almonds sounds kind of yuck, but in reality they taste pretty good.

Annemarie was still in her nightgown, but she looked normal. "My dad won't stop feeding me," she said, taking a handful of nuts. "And he won't let me get dressed. He says pajamas are good for the soul. Isn't that so dumb?"

I sat on the edge of her bed. "Is that the rose?" It was on her bedside table in a tiny silver vase, just the kind of thing they would have at Annemarie's house.

She nodded and looked at it. The rose was perfect—just opening, like a picture in a magazine.

"I tried to draw it," Annemarie said. She held out a little spiral pad of heavy white paper. She'd sketched the rose in dark pencil, over and over.

"Wow," I said. "I didn't know you could draw like that."

She flipped the pad closed. "My dad shows me tricks sometimes. There are a lot of tricks to drawing. I can show you."

But I knew I could never draw like that, for the same reason I couldn't do Jimmy's V-cut or get my Main Street diagrams to look good.

"Hey," I said, "maybe your *dad* left you the rose."

"Maybe." She frowned, and I felt a little piece of myself light up. "He says he didn't, though."

"But it would explain how the person got upstairs, why the doorman didn't buzz you." I could feel my lips making a smile. "Your dad is so nice. It has to be him."

I was miserable, sitting on the edge of her bed in that puddle of meanness. But I couldn't help it. I didn't want Annemarie's rose to be from Colin. Maybe I couldn't stand for her to have so many people, and to be able to draw and cut bread on top of that. Maybe I wanted Colin for myself.

Annemarie's dad stuck his head through the doorway. "Anybody need a refill?"

"No thanks," I said, even though my glass was empty and my back teeth were packed with chewed nuts. "I have to go."

"Stay for five more minutes," he said. "I put your coat in the dryer."

So I had to sit there, thirsty, and then I had to put on my dry, warm, but still-dirty coat and take the elevator down to Annemarie's lobby, where the lamps glowed yellow and the doorman remembered my name. It had stopped raining.

It was too cold for the boys to hang around in front of the garage. There was hardly anyone out on the street at all.

The light in Belle's window looked friendly in the late-afternoon gloom, and I thought of going in. I had been telling Belle the story of my book, a little bit here and a little bit there. I'd told her how Meg helped her father escape, and I'd described the first battle with IT, which is this giant, evil brain that wants to control everyone. I knew Belle would give me some vitamin Cs and maybe a paper cup of hot chocolate, but it was getting late and I didn't want to have to walk down our block in the complete dark, so I decided to keep going.

At first I thought the laughing man wasn't on the corner, but then I saw him sitting on the wet curb, leaning against the mailbox and just watching me walk toward him. For one second there was something familiar about him, and I noticed for the first time how old he looked. I thought about what Louisa had said, about how old people can't get enough heat. Maybe I felt sorry for him. Maybe he reminded me of Mr.

Nunzi from upstairs. Or maybe I wanted to do something good, to make up for being kind of a jerk to Annemarie, even if she didn't really know it. Anyway, I spoke to him.

"Hey," I said, opening my bag. "You want a sandwich?" I still had the cheese sandwich I hadn't eaten at lunch. I held it out. "It's cheese and tomato."

"Is it on a hard roll?" He sounded tired. "I can't eat hard bread. Bad teeth."

"It isn't hard," I said. It was one of my best V-cuts ever, probably a little soggy now with the juice from the tomato soaking into the bread all afternoon.

He reached up with one hand, and I put the sandwich in it.

"What was the burn scale today?" he asked.

"I'm not sure," I said, pretending I knew what he was talking about. "I didn't have a chance to, um, check."

"Rain is no protection," he said, looking at the sandwich in his hand. "They should have had the dome up."

"Maybe tomorrow," I said.

He looked up at me, and suddenly he seemed familiar again. It was something about the way his eyes took me in. He said, "I'm an old man, and she's gone now. So don't worry, okay?"

"I won't."

He nodded. "Smart kid."

Things That Get Stuck

"Guess what?" I said to Mom when she got home. "The laughing man isn't completely crazy. He's kind of a CSP."

"CSP?"

"Crazy-shaped person."

"Don't say 'crazy-shaped person.' And what are you talking about?"

"I gave him a sandwich today. He was sort of normal about it. Almost."

"You gave him a sandwich?"

"It was a leftover. From Jimmy's."

"Mira, why in the world would you give the laughing man a sandwich?"

"What's wrong with that? I thought you would like it!"

"You thought I would like the fact that you've struck up a relationship with a mentally ill person?"

"What relationship? I just gave him a sandwich!"

"We've talked about this, Miranda. I thought you knew how to handle yourself. It's the only reason I let you walk around alone!"

"I just gave a sandwich to a homeless guy! *You're* the one who works for criminals and hangs around with pregnant jailbirds."

"Not everyone accused of a crime is a criminal, you know. And besides, *I'm* not twelve."

I pointed at her sweatshirt, which had a rainbow on it. "Well, you *dress* like you're twelve!" I could feel the tears starting, so I grabbed two bags of the chips Louisa had brought over, went to my room, and slammed the door.

A few minutes later, she knocked and came in. "I'm sorry. You did a nice thing. I shouldn't have blown up at you like that."

"Why *did* you, then?"

She sat down on the bed next to me. "I don't know. I guess it made me nuts, thinking you were putting yourself in danger. I like to tell myself that you're always safe, but there's no such thing, really, is there? I do trust you, Mira. I want you to know that. I just—I don't want to make any more mistakes. I don't think I can bear to make one more single mistake."

"What are you talking about? What mistakes?"

She laughed. "Are you kidding? Where should I start? I've made about a million mistakes. Luckily, you outweigh almost all of them."

"*Almost* all of them? Like how many?"

She smiled. "I don't know. Nine hundred and ninety-nine thousand?"

"So that just leaves—what? A thousand to go?"

"Richard wants to move in," she said flatly. "He wants us to get married."

And my brain said, "He *does?*" Then I got this feeling of . . . lightness. I was happy. "That's great," I told Mom.

"You think so?" She smiled for a second, and then her mouth dropped. "I don't know. I just can't . . . I can't figure out if it's the right thing."

"Don't you love him?"

"Of course I do! I don't know if it's the right thing for you, I mean."

"Is that why you won't give him a key? Because of me?"

She shook her head slowly. "I don't know. I just feel stuck, like I'm afraid to take any steps, in case they're the wrong ones. I need a little more time to think." She stood up. "The water's probably boiling by now. Spaghetti in ten minutes."

Spaghetti again. We were kind of stuck, I realized. In a lot of ways.

Tied-Up Things

"You two have certainly gotten close," Mom said the following weekend while she helped me tug the roll-away cot from the overstuffed hall closet. "That's nice, right?"

Annemarie was sleeping over for the first time.

"Don't you ever vacuum?" I said. "There's dust bunnies behind all the doors."

"Give me a break, Mira," she said sharply.

"I mean it—I saw a roach in the bathroom this morning. This place looks gross."

Mom glared at me. A whole angry conversation seemed to pass over her face. Then she said, "You know what? Do this yourself," and walked away.

I pulled the cot into my room and lined it up next to my bed the way Sal and I always had. Then I wondered whether that was the way other girls did it. Was the cot supposed to be against the far wall? Should I make an L-shape with my bed, so that just our heads were together? I decided on the L-shape, stood back, adjusted the angle, and then went to get the sheets out of the bathroom closet.

* * *

Starting when we were really little, Sal and I used to beg to have sleepovers on the weekends, and lots of nights I fell asleep happy with Sal next to me on the roll-away.

But he was never there in the morning. I would wake up and see the empty cot with its tumbled-up striped sheets, and Mom would tell me what had happened—he'd woken up with a stomachache, or a headache, or a bad dream, and wanted to go home.

She'd hand me a tissue and say, "I don't know why we keep doing this. Sal cries in the middle of the night and then you cry in the morning."

A couple of weeks later, we would try again. And I always believed that *this* would be the time Sal would still be there in the morning. Eventually we stopped trying, and then those striped blue sheets made me sad to look at.

But they were the only ones we had that fit the cot. I tucked them in and went to Mom's room to take one of her pillows. She was still being angry in the living room. I fluffed the pillow, placed it carefully on the cot, and stood back. It looked okay.

I was still standing there when the buzzer rang, and I got this clear mental picture of Annemarie and her dad in our lobby with the cigarette smell and the ugly ceiling light full of dead bugs. It was like a vision, almost.

I went to the intercom and pushed the Talk button. "Who is it?"

Her dad's voice: "It's Annemarie and her unshaven father!"

I buzzed long and hard in a way that was supposed to say "you are extra welcome to be here." Also, the lobby door is so heavy I wanted to give them time to get it open.

Mom came and stood next to me by the front door, saying nothing and running her fingers through her hair. She was wearing jeans and had changed her T-shirt for a black turtleneck sweater.

It was at that moment, standing next to her, that I figured out the truth. The truth was that Mom saw it too: the peeling paint, the cigarette butts on the stairs, everything. It soaked into me like water into sand, fast and heavy-making.

But I still couldn't apologize for what I'd said. I wanted to, but I couldn't. I couldn't even smile at her.

"Welcome!" Mom sang to Annemarie's dad. "I'm so glad Annemarie can spend the night with us."

Annemarie's dad had a cardboard box full of stuff, little containers and plastic bags, which he offered to Mom. "I'm sure Miranda's mentioned that Annemarie eats a special diet," he started.

"Oh!" Mom looked at me. "Actually . . ."

"Never fear!" He pushed the box at her again. "I've brought all sorts of appropriate goodies. Feel free to sample them yourself. They're not bad, if I do say so myself!"

Mom smiled and took the box. "That's wonderful. Thanks. Had I known . . ."

"Never fear!" Annemarie's dad said again. I saw that the things inside were tied up with purple and green curly ribbon, like Christmas presents.

Annemarie and I played some records in my room, and Mom brought in a special platter with Annemarie's snacks on it, and a bowl of chips for me, and then we watched TV in the living room for a while before bed. We were watching *Love Boat* when we heard something hit the kitchen floor, followed by a bunch of cursing from Mom.

A minute later she popped her head in and looked at Annemarie. "Sorry. You didn't hear that, okay? I dropped some frozen grape juice on my foot."

Annemarie smiled a wide smile. "No problem."

"Your mom is so cool," she said later, when we were in our beds and her face was resting on Mom's pillow. "I like her a lot. She's like a real person, you know? And she treats you like a real person too. My dad still acts like I'm a baby."

"I guess."

But who wants to be treated like a real person? I thought. I wanted to be treated like Annemarie and have all my snacks tied up with ribbon.

When I opened my eyes in the morning, Annemarie was still there. I felt this big rush of relief, like I'd been worrying all night that she would disappear. Maybe I had been, without realizing it.

"Thank God you're awake!" she said, her head propped up on one arm. "I've been poking you for twenty minutes. You sleep like the dead."

"What time is it?" I asked, throwing off my blanket.

"Time to eat," she said. "I'm starved."

"Can you eat cereal?" I asked. "All I know how to make is cereal and toast."

"Nope," she said. "Can't eat either one. Got any eggs?"

We went to the kitchen to check.

"Good morning!" Mom was standing in front of the stove, making bacon. "Annemarie, I called your dad last night, and he told me that you have a thing for bacon omelets."

"Yum!" Annemarie said. "That smells great. No wonder I'm so hungry."

I was staring. Mom had serious bed head and her eyes were puffy with sleep. But she was up at seven-thirty in the morning, making us bacon omelets. I wanted to hug her. But didn't.

Things That Turn Pink

It snowed a little on the second-to-last day before Christmas vacation. Snow always puts me in a good mood. Mr. Tompkin let us skip the math workbooks and spend the whole morning on our Main Street projects. Annemarie helped me start my swings. So far, the perfect day.

By the time we walked to Jimmy's, the snow had stopped and the sidewalk was just slushy enough to make my sneakers uncomfortably wet. Mom had slept through the weather report, so I was the only one without boots.

Colin started to push open Jimmy's door, but Jimmy jumped out from behind the counter and leaned against the door so it slammed in our faces.

"Hey!" Colin smiled, thinking it was a joke, and shoved back. But I could see Jimmy's face better than Colin could. It wasn't a joke.

"Get out!" Jimmy called through the glass. "Don't come back here anymore! You're lucky I don't call the police!"

Annemarie put her hand on Colin's shoulder. "I think he's serious."

"What?" Colin saw our faces and then looked up at Jimmy through the door. "What's going on?" he yelled.

Jimmy had one foot up against the bottom of the door. He glared at us. Some people on the street looked over, but nobody stopped.

"Somebody stole my bank," he said finally, his voice sounding far away. "One of you."

Of course we told him, through the door, that we didn't, that we wouldn't. But there was no way he was letting us in.

We went to the pizza place and talked about who could have taken Jimmy's two-dollar bills. He ran the place alone, aside from the forty minutes a day that we were there. Maybe someone had run in while he was in the bathroom, we thought. He usually put his *Back in Five Minutes* sign in the window and locked the door, but not every time. Sometimes he just ran into the back for a minute and if someone came in, they waited. Someone could have taken the bank then. But who in the world would have known to take it in the first place? It was a faded plastic bank in the shape of a cartoon character. It didn't look remotely valuable.

"Let's write him a letter," Annemarie said. "Or no—we'll get him a card!" She used her spoon to scrape up the last of her lunch, which her dad packed for her every day in a cleaned-out yogurt container. "Come on," she said, standing up. "It'll be my treat."

So we went into Gold's Stationery and bought Jimmy a greeting card. I wanted to get one that said *With Sympathy,* for Jimmy's lost bank, but Annemarie said we should pick something that was blank inside. She picked a card with roses on it, which I thought was kind of strange, considering it was for Jimmy and roses are supposed to symbolize love. She said the card looked sincere, but I guessed that she liked it because it reminded her of her mystery rose.

"What do you think?" she asked Colin. She held up the card in front of him.

Colin raised his shoulders and dropped them. "I guess."

Annemarie said nothing, but she looked like she'd been hoping for a more revealing answer. "Can you put this on my dad's account?" she asked the cashier.

"Sure thing, Annemarie. Hey, where's your pal Julia? Home sick today?"

Annemarie turned pink. "No, she's around."

The cashier smiled and handed Annemarie a spiral notebook with a beaten-up cover. Annemarie flipped it open and wrote her name and the date.

A charge account at Gold's. I thought of the fat smelly markers that cost two-fifty each, the leather diaries that locked with little keys, the battery-operated fans that you could wear on a string around your neck on hot days.

"Hey, Annemarie," Colin said. "Wanna buy me a pack of baseball cards?"

She turned pink again. "I can't. I mean, I'm not allowed. Sorry."

He shrugged and smiled. "No big deal."

Sometimes I wanted to squeeze Colin's cheeks until his teeth fell out.

After school, Annemarie and I went to her house. Her dad brought us some weird kind of thin ham rolled up so we could eat it with our fingers.

We wrote on Jimmy's card:

> Dear Jimmy,
> We did not take your Fred
> Flintstone bank. We don't know
> who could have taken it (maybe
> someone came in when you
> went to the bathroom?).
> Can we come back to work?
>
> Signed,
> Your employees,
> Annemarie, Miranda, and Colin

I put the card in my knapsack so that I could slip it under Jimmy's door the next morning on my way to school. Then we lay on Annemarie's rug and planned all the stuff we were going to do over Christmas vacation: Annemarie wanted to start teaching me how to draw, even though I told her I was probably hopeless, and we were going to go to the movies, and her dad even said he would take us ice-skating in Central Park.

I tried not to wonder what Sal would be doing. I figured he'd be playing basketball right up until the first big snow.

Things That Fall Apart

The next morning on my way to school, I pushed our card under Jimmy's locked door. At lunchtime, Colin, Annemarie, and I walked up to Broadway together. Jimmy was helping a customer, but he saw us through the glass door, made a face, and shook his head no.

"I guess he means it," Colin said.

We stood there in front of the door for a minute, just in case. When the customer left with his sandwich, Jimmy glanced over at us again. Colin put his hands together under his chin like he was praying and made a puppy-dog face, which was a dumb joke but also pretty cute. Jimmy took a rag and started wiping down the counter, and then he raised one arm and waved us in without looking up.

"So we can come back to work?" Colin asked when we'd all crowded in the door.

Jimmy looked at us. "You're good kids," he said, "but you don't know what you're doing half the time."

"We didn't take the bank!" I started, and he waved at me to be quiet.

"I know. I been thinking about it. You can come back to work."

"Yay!" Annemarie started clapping. Colin ran around slapping everyone five, including Jimmy, who even smiled.

"But here's the thing," Jimmy said after Colin had taken a victory lap behind the counter and through the back room. "Your friend, little Swiss Miss. Don't let me find her in here again. Ever."

"Who?" Annemarie said.

"I think he means Julia," I said.

"You think Julia took the money?" Colin laughed. "Julia needs money like a fish needs a bicycle."

Jimmy shook his head. "Some things are in the blood. All the money in the world can't change a person's blood."

"What do you mean, 'blood'?" Annemarie had her hands on her hips. "What blood?"

Jimmy pointed his big finger right at me. "Like you call her, Swiss Miss: hot chocolate."

"Huh?" Colin looked at me and back to Jimmy. I was just getting it. Annemarie was way ahead of me.

"You . . . you *pig*," she said. "You racist pig." I had never seen Annemarie angry. She was scary and also obviously about to cry.

Jimmy shrugged. "It's your life. I'm not having that little thief back in here. You don't have to come back either."

"I won't!" Annemarie shouted, and she banged out the door.

"And that's not why I call her Swiss Miss!" I said.

Jimmy shrugged again, and I banged out after Annemarie. Colin followed me. We found her crying halfway down the block, walking fast.

She was spitting words: "That. Big. Fat. Jerk. That. Pig. I. Hate. Him."

Colin looked at me. "I don't even get what just happened!"

Annemarie whirled around to face us. "He thinks Julia did it because she's black."

"No way," Colin said. "He's crazy."

Annemarie turned on me then. "Is that your name for her? Swiss Miss?"

"I—no! I said it one time, but I didn't mean . . . I meant about how she's always talking about Switzerland, her watch and the chocolate, and—"

"She is?" Colin asked. "I never heard her talk about Switzerland."

"If anyone needs the money," Annemarie said to me coldly, "it's you, not Julia."

"Are you serious? I didn't take the stupid money!"

"Forget it," she said. "I want to be alone." And she stomped off toward school.

Colin raised his eyebrows after her and then showed me a rolled-up dollar. "Want to get a slice?"

So we went to the pizza place. But it wasn't fun. And walking back to school, it occurred to me that Colin might not like me at all. He might just like pizza.

"Tell me something," I said just before we got to

our classroom. "That day the bread count was short by two rolls. Did you take them?"

"Yeah," Colin said, starting to smile. "I thought it would be . . . Hey! I didn't steal Jimmy's bank, you know!" He looked at me through his bangs with his injured-puppy face.

"I know," I said quickly. "I know you wouldn't."

"The rolls were just for fun," he said. "But taking the bank would be, you know, *stealing*."

"Yeah."

I didn't get to talk to Annemarie all the rest of that afternoon. After silent reading period, she went to art and music, and I went to gym and science. And then some of the kindergartners came to our classroom to sing "Rudolph the Red-Nosed Reindeer."

And then it was Christmas vacation.

Christmas Vacation

For three days in a row, the sky was like a dingy white sheet. I thought about calling Annemarie but didn't. I thought about calling Colin but didn't. I was right about Sal—he was playing basketball every day, and a couple of times there were the voices of other boys, kids from school. On the third day, I opened our living room window very quietly and watched them running up and down the alley in their knit hats with steam blowing out of their mouths.

Then I sat on the couch and closed my eyes. I pictured the world. I pictured the world millions of years ago, with crazy clouds of gas everywhere, and volcanoes, and the continents bumping into each other and then drifting apart. Okay. Now life begins. It starts in the water, with tiny things, microscopic, and then some get bigger. And one day something crawls out of the water onto land. There are animals, then humans, looking almost all alike. There are tiny differences in color, the shape of the face, the tone of the skin. But basically they are the same. They create shelters, grow food, experiment. They talk; they write things down.

Now fast-forward. The earth is still making loops around the sun. There are humans all over the place, driving in cars and flying in airplanes. And then one day one human tells another human that he doesn't want to walk to school with her anymore.

"Does it really matter?" I asked myself.

It did.

I tried again. I pictured the world, all pretty blue-green and floating out in space, creatures and forests and deserts and cities. I brought North America into focus, the United States, the East Coast, New York City. Kids are walking down the street toward school. One kid has green suede boots. One has a charge account at Gold's. One has keys in her pocket.

"Does it really matter?" I asked myself.

It did.

I got up, turned on the television, and tried to think about nothing for a change.

The Second Proof

Mom didn't have to work on Christmas Eve day. We got a tree and strung popcorn for it, and she had some friends from work over. Richard made some eggnog from a German recipe his grandmother gave him, and they all ended up singing a lot while I wrapped presents in my room. I had bought Mom a pair of earrings, a bottle of purple nail polish with glitter in it, and some striped tights, even though I thought, and I still think, that striped tights look dumb. I got Richard an erasable pen from Gold's.

On Christmas morning, we opened presents first thing after Mom made coffee, like always. I got some good stuff: a beaded bracelet, a portable radio, a fancy journal to write in with clouds on the cover, a sweater, and a tin of these really crispy ginger cookies I love from a bakery near Mom and Richard's office.

We were just about to move on to pancakes when Richard handed me a hard, rectangular package that had to be a book.

"Let me guess," I said. "A book?" I wondered if it would be the kind with a spunky girl on the cover.

"Very funny. Open it."

It was a book. Actually, it was *my* book. But this was a hardcover one, with a different picture on the front. I read the title out loud: *"A Wrinkle in Time."* And then I smiled at Richard.

"It's a first edition," Richard said.

"Richard!" Mom burst out. "You shouldn't have." This made me guess that first editions are expensive.

"Read what's inside," he said. "I had the author sign it for you."

I opened the front cover. The writing was big and swoopy, beautiful. Nothing like yours.

Miranda,
Tesser well.
Madeleine L'Engle

Christmas Day: *Tesser well.* Your second proof.

It wasn't a game, I realized. Holding that book in my hands, I finally believed that whoever wrote me those notes actually knew about things before they happened. Somehow.

As soon as Richard and Mom went to make the pancakes, I ran to my room and took all your notes out of the box under my bed.

I am coming to save your friend's life, and my own.

Coming from where? I asked myself. Coming from *when?* I was beginning to believe that someone I cared about was in real danger, but I still didn't know who it was, and I still didn't know how to help.

I looked at the second note: *I know you have shared my first note. I ask you not to share the others. Please. I do not ask this for myself.*

That was the worst part: I was alone.

Things in an Elevator

New Year's Day was weirdly warm and sunny. Sal's basketball was going strong by about nine in the morning. I sneaked a look down into the alley and saw him running back and forth in just a T-shirt and a pair of sweatpants. He was wearing the watch Louisa had given him for Christmas. She'd come up to show it to us beforehand. It was kind of old-fashioned, with Roman numerals and a leather band, and I hadn't been sure Sal would like it. But it looked like he did.

Mom was sleeping late. I wrote her a note: *I went out. I'll get you a bagel.*

The laughing man wasn't on the corner—maybe he didn't work holidays. Belle's was closed. Everything felt kind of peaceful and sad and deserted.

My feet carried me to school, which was closed, of course. The yard gate was open, and I went in and sat on the jungle gym for a few minutes, letting myself feel how strange it was to be there alone. I was sort of deliberately trying to weird myself out, I think, to get my energy up. To call Annemarie.

Ten days of silence had grown into a question that my brain shouted inside my head: "Is Annemarie even your friend anymore?" There was a pay phone on the corner. I had a dime in my coat.

As I dialed, I noticed someone leaning over the garbage can across the street. When he pulled himself upright I saw it was the laughing man. He stood there with his hands on his hips looking down at the garbage. I quickly turned my back to him, worried that he might recognize me and come over.

The receiver of the pay phone was cold against my ear. Only after it started ringing did it occur to me that if my mother was sleeping, Annemarie's parents might be sleeping too.

"*Yello!*" Annemarie's dad answered the phone. He sounded as if he'd been up for hours, just sitting by the phone and hoping, hoping, hoping it would ring.

"Hi . . . it's Miranda—"

"Hi, Miranda! Happy New Year!"

"Hi. I mean, Happy New Year to you too. I was wondering if Annemarie is there."

"She is! But she's in the shower. Are you by any chance outside, Miranda? It sounds like you might be at a pay phone."

"Oh. Yeah, I am, actually."

"In the neighborhood?"

"Um, yeah. I'm right by school."

"Well, come on over. I'm pouring you some orange juice right now!"

"Uh, okay."

"You can surprise Annemarie!"

Would I ever. I walked up the hill, where the sun-light seemed to touch everything like it was a hyper kid running all over a toy store—it bounced off the dirty metal lampposts, the shiny brass awning posts, even the sunglasses of a woman walking her dogs with a cup of coffee in one hand. Everything *shined*.

"Miss Miranda, Happy New Year!" Annemarie's door-man was standing just outside the building's polished doors. He smiled and waved me in.

On the way up, it hit me that it was truly strange to come over here without talking to Annemarie first. But at the exact same time I got nervous about that, I also got this other feeling, which I can only describe as love for Annemarie's elevator. The wood paneling, the cloth-covered stool in one corner, the little bell that went off every time we passed another floor. It was all so nice and cozy that I thought it would be wonderful to stay inside it forever, or at least to sit down on the little stool and close my eyes for a while. The whole thing was beyond weird. And then the elevator stopped on Annemarie's floor, and of course I got out, because that's what people do when the elevator gets to their floor.

Annemarie answered the door in her robe, with wet hair.

"Hi," I started. "I just called to say Happy New Year, and your dad said—"

She smiled. "Come on in."

It was the best morning. Annemarie showed me her Christmas presents. She got all kinds of cool art stuff, and we ended up spreading it all over the dining room table and drawing comic strips on this special comic-strip paper that came with stickers for the talking bubbles and the thinking bubbles. And then her mom showed us how to make origami frogs, and I was actually good at it. Meanwhile, her dad kept bringing in these plates of bacon and, for me, French toast strips I could pick up with my hands.

Then Mom called. I had completely forgotten about her. She was frantic, she was angry, and she was coming to get me. Even Annemarie's dad looked mad.

"Better get your coat on," he said when I hung up the phone, even though my mom couldn't possibly get to Annemarie's apartment that fast. So I waited by the door, overheating in my coat, and Annemarie waited with me.

"So, about what happened at Jimmy's . . . ," I said. "You know, I really never meant . . . what he thought I meant. Not for one second."

She looked at the floor. "I totally believe you. And I don't know why I said that thing I said, about . . . money. It was stupid."

"It's okay." I was so grateful that she had something to apologize for that it didn't really occur to me to think about how it had actually made me feel. But I have thought about it since then. It didn't make me feel good.

*   *   *

We heard the elevator's ding and I opened Annemarie's front door before Mom had a chance to ring the bell. I thought I might be able to escape without Annemarie's parents talking to her.

No such luck. "Jerry?" Mom called out, and Annemarie's dad came rushing over saying, "Oh, you're here. I didn't hear the bell—"

"I'm so sorry about this," Mom said.

"No, *I'm* sorry. I had no idea—"

"It'll never happen again—"

"—always check with you first."

They cross-talked for a while, then hit one of those natural breaks in the conversation and both turned to look at me.

"Let's go," Mom said coldly, and I said, "Thanks for having me," and Annemarie's dad smiled at me, but only because he's the nicest person on earth.

The elevator opened right away, so there was no awkward waiting. On the way down, I knew I should apologize, but I just waited for Mom to jump all over me. Instead she burst into tears.

Which made me cry. So we both cried through the lobby, past the doorman, and out into the sunlight, where we magically stopped. She took a deep breath and looked at me. "I was scared," she said. "When you didn't come back, I got really scared. Don't ever do that again."

I nodded.

"Okay," she said. "What now?"

"I don't know."

"Maybe a movie?"

So that's what we did. We went to the movies, and ate candy and popcorn, and held hands for a few minutes on the way home.

The laughing man was at his regular post, doing his kicks into the street. When he saw us he yelled, "Smart kid!" But having Mom there made it different, like walking down the street with a blanket wrapped tight around me.

Richard was leaning up against our building, reading a newspaper.

"Hey!" he said. "We had a plan. Did you forget about me?"

He made a sad face, and Mom said, "Oh, no! How late am I?" and then she looked at me and we both started laughing.

Richard said, "Seriously. Would it kill you to give me a key?" And Mom shrugged and said it was only three-thirty and she didn't much feel like going upstairs anyway. So we turned around and went to eat at the diner, which was full of people just waking up and having breakfast.

Things You Realize

It was 1979—a new year, a new decade, almost, but school was still just school. Jay Stringer was still a genius, music assemblies were still boring, and Alice Evans was still too shy to admit when she had to go to the bathroom. The fourth grade's violin performance had only just started, and already Alice was squirming in her seat next to me. Jay was on my other side, somehow reading a book while listening to the world's worst music.

I located Sal's blond head a few rows ahead on my right. I stared at the back of it for a while, trying to see if I could make him turn around with the sheer power of my brain waves, but it was hard to concentrate with Alice doing a Mexican hat dance in her chair. I tried to make a face at Annemarie, who was on the other side of Alice, but Annemarie seemed fully absorbed by the music. She's extremely nonjudgmental that way. So I went back to looking at Sal.

Directly in front of me was Julia. She was obviously as bored as I was—her head kept bobbing around. And then she turned and looked at Annemarie. I glanced over and saw that Annemarie's eyes were still on the stage. Julia watched Annemarie. And I watched Julia watching Annemarie. And what I saw were eyes that were sixty-percent-cacao chocolate, a face that was café au lait, and an expression that was so familiar it made my whole body ring like a bell. Julia's look was my look. My looking at Sal.

And suddenly I knew three things:

First, it was Julia who had left the rose for Annemarie.

Second, Julia cared about Annemarie, but Annemarie didn't see it. Because I was standing in the way.

Third, Alice Evans was about to pee in her pants.

I turned to Alice. "Hey," I said, "I have to go to the bathroom. Be my partner?"

Sometimes you never feel meaner than the moment you stop being mean. It's like how turning on a light makes you realize how dark the room had gotten. And the way you usually act, the things you would have normally done, are like these ghosts that everyone can see but pretends not to. It was like that when I asked Alice Evans to be my bathroom partner. I wasn't one of the girls who tortured her on purpose, but I had never lifted a finger to help her before, or even spent one minute being nice to her.

She stopped squirming and looked at me suspiciously. "You have to go?" she said. "Really?"

"Yeah." And in that moment, I wanted nothing as much as I wanted Alice to feel safe with me. "Really."

I leaned forward in my seat and waved my arm up and down so that Mr. Tompkin turned to look at me from his seat at the end of the row, and I spoke over the laps of Jay Stringer and Colin, who were sitting between us.

"I have to go to the bathroom." These words felt like some kind of sacrifice, a precious offering to the universe. I didn't know why, but Julia's look had given me this total determination to get Alice Evans to the bathroom before she wet herself.

"*Now?*" Mr. Tompkin whispered.

"Please!"

He rolled his eyes. "Fine."

Mr. Tompkin tilted his knees to one side to let us pass, and Jay Stringer and Colin put their heads together and then Jay laughed. My mind processed that—if Jay was the one who'd laughed, then Colin was the one who'd made the joke. A joke about me, maybe. I grabbed Alice's hand and pulled her after me. And then we were running up the aisle.

Things You Beg For

As soon as Alice went into the bathroom, I ran down the hall toward the office. There were so many things I wanted to do but couldn't, like hug my mom, or be less jealous of Annemarie, and I didn't want this to become one of them. But I had to work fast.

"Miranda?" Wheelie looked up at me doubtfully. "Aren't you supposed to be in assembly?"

"Yes, I am in assembly—I mean, I was, and I'm going right back. Alice is in the bathroom. Can I have a piece of paper?"

"No, ma'am! I don't have paper to be just giving away."

"Please—just a little piece. A corner of a piece!" If I didn't do this now, I never would.

Wheelie sighed. Then, still in her chair, she kicked her way over to the next desk, where there was one of those pink message pads. She ripped off the top sheet, folded it, folded it again, and then carefully ripped the paper along the first fold, and then along the second fold. "Hurry," my brain said. "Hurry."

"Here." She held out a quarter of a pink message slip and looked at me with a face that said "I hope you won't be coming around here looking for another handout anytime soon."

I picked up a pen from the counter and scribbled on the little pink square.

"I thought you left me." Alice was standing in front of the bathroom looking all wounded.

"Me?" I said. "No way."

She smiled. People seemed to like the new me.

We squeezed back into our row past Colin and Jay Stringer, who whispered and laughed again. Annemarie leaned forward and gave me a where-were-you shrug. I mouthed "Bathroom," and she nodded and settled back again.

I folded my pink square a couple of times. Then I leaned forward and dropped the note into Julia's lap. I hadn't had much time—it was just the one word: TRUCE.

And underneath I'd written my phone number.

Things That
Turn Upside Down

That afternoon, Sal brought Colin home after school. I saw them up ahead of me, taking turns on Colin's skateboard. One would ride, and the other would bounce Sal's basketball—they were circling each other and laughing and racing around and I wanted to be part of it so much that my heart almost broke watching. I decided to stop off at Belle's.

Belle picked up the economy jug of chewable vitamin C she kept behind the register and shook it at me. I nodded, and she tipped four of them into my hand.

"What's up?" she asked.

"Not much."

"Got some time for the story?"

"Sure. Where were we?"

"Aunt Beast."

"Right. Aunt Beast. So Aunt Beast's planet is perfect—it smells great and the food is wonderful and everything is soft and comfortable. But Meg can't stay there. She has to go back and save her little brother. They left him behind, with IT, remember?"

Belle nodded. "She has to go back by herself?"

"Yes. She's the only one who can do it, because she's closer to her brother than anyone. It has to be her."

Belle nodded.

"So she goes back there, to Camazotz, and her brother is totally under ITs control, and he's saying all these awful things to her. And IT is trying to suck her in too, to take over her brain. She's trying to resist, but it's hard. And then, at the last second, she figures out that there's only one thing that can defeat IT: love. IT doesn't understand love."

"Ooh," Belle said. "That's deep."

"So Meg stands there and thinks about how much she loves her brother—her *real* brother, not the IT-brother who is standing there with his mouth hanging open and his eyes twirling. She starts yelling over and over that she loves him, and poof, he becomes himself again. That's how she saves him. It turns out to be really simple."

Belle surprised me. "Well, it's simple to love someone," she said. "But it's hard to know when you need to say it out loud."

For some reason that made me want to cry. "Anyway," I said. "Then they're suddenly back home. They land in the vegetable garden outside their house, in the broccoli. That's the end."

Of course I couldn't help thinking of what Marcus had said, about how if they'd gotten home five minutes before they left, they would have seen themselves get back home before they even knew they were going. But it was better not to drag Belle into all that.

"What's the name of this writer again?"

I spelled it out for her.

Belle had to ring up a few kids buying their after-school junk food, so I wandered around the store. I was thinking I would swipe a few grapes, but they looked old and soft. I took a bottle of chocolate milk out of the refrigerator, checked the date on it, and brought it up to the register with a five-dollar bill I had taken from Mom's coat pocket that morning.

"Weirdest thing," Belle said, taking my five. "You see that guy out there?" She pointed through her front window and across the street to where the laughing man was pacing back and forth on my corner, doing his kicks.

"Yeah."

"Well, check this out." She lifted the plastic tray out of the register drawer, and I looked in. It was full of two-dollar bills. Wavy, bent-looking two-dollar bills.

"A couple weeks ago, that guy out there suddenly starts coming in every day to get a butter-on-white and a banana, and he always pays with these two-dollar bills."

I was staring into the drawer.

"You want a couple for your change?" Belle asked.

I nodded, and she handed them to me. "Sorry," she said, smoothing them out, "they're crumpled. He gives them to me all folded up into triangles, if you can believe it. The first time, I didn't even think it was real money. I started telling the guy to get lost!"

My brain was doing that thing where it yells at me. It was yelling, "The *laughing man* stole Jimmy's Fred Flintstone bank? The *laughing man?*"

"The guy is looney," Belle said thoughtfully, "but also generally polite. Polite is always worth something."

When I walked by him a minute later, the laughing man was shaking his fist at the sky and kicking his legs out into the traffic rushing up Amsterdam Avenue. A few cars honked at him. When he saw me, he pointed and yelled, "Smart kid! Smart kid!"

I popped my last two vitamin Cs and imagined the wrapped-in-a-blanket feeling I'd had when Mom was with me. Then I calmly walked by the laughing man, thinking, Yeah, really polite.

Colin and Sal were in the lobby, making a total racket with the skateboard and the basketball so that any second Mrs. Bindocker would probably come charging out of her apartment, yelling that they were scaring her cat.

"Hey!" Colin said when he saw me. "I *thought* you lived in this building. Want to skate a little?" He picked up his skateboard and held it out to me.

I glanced at Sal, who was concentrating on his basketball like the whole concept of bouncing had just been invented and was really very amazing and deserving of attention. He had developed a way of waving at me without making eye contact—it was kind of like a no-look pass.

"No thanks," I said, "I have to go."

But Colin is Colin. If he can read a vibe, he never lets on. "Can I see your place?" he said. "We're shooting baskets in the back—have you been back there? It's cool. Want to come hang out?"

I told Colin that my mother was sick upstairs, and that I was just rushing home from the store.

"You got her chocolate milk?" he asked, pointing at the bottle in my hand.

"Yeah." I headed for the stairs. "She loves it." And I sprinted up to the second floor before he could say anything else.

When I unlocked our door, the apartment felt like a warm hug—the refrigerator was humming, the light was streaming through the living room windows, and the voice in my head said "Safe" and then got quiet. I went to the kitchen, opened my chocolate milk, and took the last bag of Lay's. Those pregnant jailbirds were out of luck.

Then the phone rang.

"Hello?"

"Have I reached the Sinclair residence? May I please speak with Miranda?"

I rolled my eyes. "Hi, Julia," I said. "It's me."

That first time, we only talked for five minutes. Julia said her mom had a recipe for a flourless cake we could make for Annemarie's birthday. Without knowing whether I really wanted to, I agreed to go over and make a practice cake with her after school the next day.

It was dark outside when there was a tap at the door. I sat up on the couch. A tap on the door was a strange thing. Everyone rings our doorbell, except for Louisa, who always knocks her regular knock. I was afraid— your notes had done that to me.

Another tap.

"Hello?" I called.

Silence. I got up and looked through the peephole.

Colin stood there, holding his skateboard in front of him like a shield, looking not exactly like himself.

I opened the door. "What's wrong?"

He took two steps forward and kind of hovered right in front of me for a second, and then he kissed me. And then he stopped and waited. And then I kissed him back. He smiled and ran down the stairs.

There are days when everything changes, and this was one of those days.

Things That Are Sweet

Julia's mother had a whole shelf full of books about cooking: *No-Fat Cooking, Cooking Extra-Extra-Light, Skinny Cooking.*

"My mom is *always* on a diet," Julia said, pulling a book from the shelf. "I think she bought this one by mistake. It actually has the word 'butter' in it." She laughed and held out the giant bag of Fritos she had bought on the way home.

I shook my head. I'd eaten too many already. "Should we start making the cake?"

I had to call Mom at work three times to ask her questions like how many tablespoons are there in a stick of butter, and is it okay to use a potato peeler to skin an apple. The third time I called, she said, "Hold on, Mira. Are you planning to use the oven? Is there an adult in the house?"

When I said I thought Julia's mother was home, though technically I had not actually seen her, Mom said, "But is she watching you? Where is she?"

"Where's your mother?" I whispered to Julia.

"She's meditating," Julia said.

"Here?"

"Yes—in the . . . closet. And she absolutely cannot be disturbed."

"Um—did you just say your mom's in the closet?"

Julia looked down at the French pot holder in her hand. "It's a walk-in closet," she said quietly.

Mom said we couldn't light the oven until Julia's mother came out to supervise us, so we put our clumped-together cake batter in the fridge and went to Julia's room to watch television.

Julia's room was like a ruffled version of Annemarie's—ruffled curtains, ruffled bedspread, lots of ruffled pillows. And books all over the floor, some stacked in piles, some worn-looking, some brand-new, some splayed upside down, some sliding off the pink bedside table next to the lamp with the orange fabric shade.

I tried to think of something to say about all the ruffles. "Nice lamp," I said.

She put her hands on her hips and looked at the lamp. "Really? Because I think it's kind of ugly. My mom picked it." She waved one arm across the room. "She picked out all this stuff. And she won't let me put up my outer-space posters. I had to hang them in my bathroom!" She jerked a thumb toward a door. Her own *bathroom*.

Something very familiar caught my eye. It was on the bedside table, under the ugly lamp. It was *my book*—or maybe it was my book's twin sister, just as old and beat-up-looking as mine, but with different creases and one corner ripped off the cover. I went over and picked it up.

"Yeah," she said. "I notice you carry yours around. I leave mine at home."

"I got a first edition for Christmas. That means it's one of the original—"

"You *did*? You are *so* lucky," she said. "All I ever get is clothes. And jewelry."

I stared at her. "I thought you liked all that stuff," I said.

"Yeah, actually, I do." She smiled. "But I like other stuff too." That was when I noticed her *Mysteries of Science* poster leaning up against a wall. Hers was called "Is There Intelligent Life in Outer Space?" Her bubble letters were a lot better than mine.

She flopped down on her shaggy pink wall-to-wall carpeting, glanced at her digital clock, and reached out automatically to turn on the TV. And I realized that we probably spent our afternoons the same exact way. Except I can at least get my mother on the phone. Julia's apartment is a lot nicer than ours, but I'm pretty sure there's no phone in the closet.

I stretched out on the rug and rested my head on my arm. Julia looked me up and down. "Hey, you know what color your hair is?" she asked.

"My hair?" I touched it and made a face. "It's brown."

She looked at it thoughtfully. "No. When you see it in the light, it's really more of a caramel."

Caramel.

The Last Note

I'm up to the part about what happened on the corner. If I ever do write your letter, I'll tell this part very carefully.

1. I was walking home alone after school, thinking about what to get Annemarie for her birthday.
2. It was cold but not too cold—the boys were standing outside the garage making noise, as usual. They were also throwing potato chips at each other.
3. Sal's class must have been dismissed a few minutes before mine—he was walking a little ahead of me. I did not run to catch up.
4. I watched him pass the boys outside the garage; they said some stuff to him like they sometimes do. I saw a couple of potato chips hit him on the back.
5. Sal seemed to lose it. He turned and screamed "Shut up!" He was wearing his dark blue knit cap pulled down over his forehead again.
6. The boys just laughed. My heart started going

very fast, but I wasn't really worried they would hit Sal because it is officially beneath them to hit smaller kids. Torment, yes. Hit, no.

7. One of them reached out and pushed Sal in the chest—not too hard, but Sal stumbled back a few steps. He yelled, "Jerks!" and the boys all cracked up, but no one else touched him.

8. Sal pointed himself toward home and started walking again.

9. Marcus came walking out through the dented metal door next to the garage.

10. Sal saw Marcus and broke into a run.

11. Marcus yelled, "Hold up!" and started running after Sal.

12. I saw the laughing man, across the street on the corner. He was in his nutcracker position, facing us.

13. Marcus was catching up to Sal, yelling, "Hold up! Wait!"

14. This is where things got weird: I saw something next to the laughing man, like an old movie that flickered for just a few seconds and then went out. It was between two parked cars, and it looked like a man holding his head in his hands. He was naked. And then he was gone.

15. Sal kept running. Marcus kept running. I started running.

16. "Hey! Hey—kid!" Marcus yelled. Naturally he had forgotten Sal's name.

17. Sal took one look over his shoulder and started moving faster. He was almost to the corner. Traffic was flying by on Amsterdam Avenue.

18. "Sal!" I screamed. "Stop!" But he didn't stop.

19. "Wait!" Marcus yelled. "I want to—" Then he finally seemed to figure out that Sal was running away from *him*. He slowed down. "Hey, look out!"

20. Sal was in the street, still running and looking back over his shoulder.

21. I caught up to Marcus. I think we both saw the truck at the same time. It was a big truck, moving fast.

22. "Stop!" Marcus shrieked at Sal. He was pointing at the truck with both hands. "Watch out! Watch out!"

23. I have no idea what the truck driver was doing— checking his delivery list, maybe, or changing the radio station—but he didn't see Sal in the middle of the street, and he didn't slow down.

24. I started screaming and covered my ears. I always cover my ears when I don't want something to happen, like if I drop a glass and don't want it to break. I wonder why I don't cover my eyes or my mouth. Or try to catch the glass.

25. I saw Sal's head start to turn, and I knew the exact moment he registered the truck. It was practically on top of him. Going forward meant getting hit. He was moving too fast to turn

back. Stopping on a dime might have saved him, but there was no way he could do it.

26. My brain boomed inside my head: "Sal is going to die."

27. "SAL IS GOING TO DIE."

28. SAL
IS
GOING
TO
DIE.

29. Suddenly, the laughing man was in the street, his right leg flying out in a mighty kick.

30. The laughing man's foot hit Sal's body.

31. Sal flew backward and hit the ground, hard.

32. The truck hit the laughing man.

33. Marcus sat down on the ground and started crying like there was no tomorrow. Really sobbing his head off.

34. I ran over to where Sal was lying very still with his arm tucked underneath him in a way that was not right. "Sal!" I screamed. "Sal!" He looked dead.

35. The truck made a long screeching noise, and then the driver came running out and shoved me away from Sal.

36. Someone (I found out later it was Belle) led me past a heap of something awful in the street, saying, "Don't look don't look don't look." She walked me over to the curb and sort of propped me up next to the mailbox on

our corner, and then she ran back to where the truck driver was hunched over Sal, doing something to his body. There was a shoe lying upside down at my feet.

37. I found myself staring and staring at the shoe. It was a black shoe with a two-inch platform nailed to the bottom. It was Richard's shoe.

38. Everything started to spin. I closed my eyes and leaned my head back against the cold metal of the mailbox. When I opened my eyes, I was staring at four words scratched into the blue mailbox paint. They were stacked one on top of another:

Book

Bag

Pocket

Shoe

39. "Book," "Bag," "Pocket," "Shoe." I read the words over and over. And then my brain showed me some pictures. I saw the school-library book with your first note sticking out of it. I saw the tall paper bag full of bread that hid your second note. I saw your third note, pulled out of my coat pocket with last winter's dirty tissues. And then my brain pointed my eyes at the shoe lying upside down at my feet. The shoe that had been stolen from our apartment.

40. I reached down, picked it up, and slowly turned it over. Inside was a small square of stiff paper just like the first three:

> This is the story I need you to tell. This and everything that has led up to it.
>
> Please deliver your letter by hand. You know where to find me.
>
> My apologies for the terse instructions. The trip is a difficult one; I can carry nothing, and a man can only hold so much paper in his mouth.

41. I heard Sal cry out, and looked up. The truck driver was on his knees next to Sal, saying, "Thank God, thank God, thank God, it's a miracle."

42. On the other side of the street I saw Marcus, still hunched over on the curb and crying hard. I could see him shaking. Behind him stood the boys from the garage, so still and silent that they looked like a picture of themselves.

43. Sal was not dead. The laughing man saved his life.

44. *You* saved Sal's life.

45. You were the laughing man.

46. You were the heap of something awful.

47. You are dead.

Difficult Things

That night, Richard stayed with me while Mom kept Louisa company at the hospital. Sal had a broken arm and three broken ribs, and he had to spend the night for observation.

Richard ordered a pizza. "Do you feel like talking?" he asked.

"Not really," I said. "Maybe later."

He nodded. "Just let me know."

After dinner, I closed my door and sat on my bed with your notes spread out in front of me. "Think," my brain said. "Think, think, *think*." I got out my ropes, tied some knots, and tried to start at the beginning.

The trip is a difficult one. I will not be myself when I reach you.

The trip is a difficult one, and I must ask my favors while my mind is sound.

And then there was the strangest line of all: *The trip is a difficult one; I can carry nothing, and a man can only hold so much paper in his mouth.*

I fingered the notes, so small and brittle. Had you carried them in your *mouth*?

The trip is a difficult one.

Difficult enough to scramble a person's mind and leave him raving on a street corner? What kind of a trip did that to someone? Who would deliberately *take* a trip like that?

My mind began a little chant: "And why? Why, why, *why*?"

To save Sal. That's why you stood on our corner day after day. That's why you were always doing those kicks into the street—you were *practicing*. It was all to save Sal. Because, somehow, you knew.

Time travel is possible, Marcus said. In theory.

I am coming to save your friend's life, and my own.

"Well," I said out loud to no one, "you saved Sal's life, but you failed miserably with goal number two."

Richard knocked on the door, and I jumped.

"Sorry," he said. "Didn't mean to scare you. I thought you might want to come out and have some grapes."

Richard had brought me grapes. We watched some TV and ate a giant bowl of the most perfect tart green grapes in the world. They were definitely not from Belle's.

It was nice, just sitting there watching TV together. My brain stopped asking me questions. I saw Richard glance over at me a couple of times, but he didn't ask me any questions either. And that was nice, too.

When I fell asleep on the couch, Richard turned the TV off and said I should go to bed. But once everything was quiet, I couldn't sleep. Your words were swimming in my head.

Please deliver your letter by hand. You know where to find me.

Louisa had told me that some of her old people died with nothing and no one. She said they were buried on an island somewhere north of Manhattan. I figured that was where you would be soon.

I was still worrying and feeling a little frozen when my bedroom door opened and Mom came over and sat on the edge of my bed.

"Sal is going to be fine," she whispered, putting one arm around me. "The tests are done. He'll probably be home in the morning."

I didn't say anything. I was afraid that if I spoke, I would tell her too much—I would tell her about the notes, Richard's shoes, the two-dollar bills, everything. And I thought that if I did tell her, somehow Sal might not be okay anymore. So instead I just held on to Mom's arm, and she stayed right there until I fell asleep.

Things That Heal

The next night after dinner, Mom and I went to visit Sal and Louisa downstairs. It was strange to be there, in a place I knew so well but hadn't seen in so long—like how it might feel to look at my own face in the mirror for the first time in months.

Sal was sitting up in bed with one arm in a cast. Mom gave him a careful hug, and then she and Louisa went to talk in the kitchen. Louisa had dragged a table over to the left side of Sal's bed so that he could reach it with his good arm, and there was a stack of sports magazines and stuff on it.

"Wow," I said, "are those Tootsie Pops? Your mom went all out."

He smiled, actually looking me in the eyes. "Yesterday at the hospital she brought me McDonald's," he said.

"*McDonald's?*" Louisa thought that McDonald's was a giant conspiracy against the health of all Americans. "Oh, my God. I mean, why aren't you *dead?*"

But that was a little too close to what had actually happened. He laughed, but I felt myself go red.

With his good hand, Sal shook the bag of Tootsie Pops out onto the table, found a purple one, and held it out to me. "Grape," he said.

"Aw, you remember."

But somehow that was also too close to the truth. I felt my head kind of buzz and was pretty sure I had gone red again.

"I remember everything," he said cheerfully. He seemed to be in a great mood. He also seemed to have forgotten that we weren't really friends anymore.

"You do?" I said, unwrapping my Tootsie Pop. "So do you remember why you don't like me anymore?" I was surprised to hear myself ask, but once I had, I really wanted to know the answer.

"I still like you! Of course I still like you. I just needed to—I don't know, take a break for a while. Ha! *Break*." He gestured to his sling. "Get it?" He giggled.

"But why? *I* wasn't the one who hit you!"

He shook his head. "Hit me when? What are you talking about?"

"What do you *think* I'm talking about? The day Marcus hit you. The day you bled all over your Yankees jacket—the day you shut me out!"

"Wait—who's Marcus?"

I suddenly got how totally stupid I'd been, never telling Sal that Marcus was an okay kid. I thought of the day I'd seen Sal drop to the ground and pretend to tie his shoe. He probably worried about seeing Marcus on that block every single day. He probably woke up in the morning thinking about it. And I could have done something to fix it, a long time ago.

"Marcus is the kid who hit you that day on the street. The kid you were running from yester—"

"Oh!" Sal cut me off. He looked at his feet, which were just a bump under the covers. "Yeah, that kid freaks me out. He has it in for me."

"He doesn't have it in for you," I said. "He really doesn't. I think he was trying to apologize yesterday."

He shrugged. "If you say so." He looked at me. "But that has nothing to do with—with you and me. Really."

"But the day Marcus hit you—that was the day that you stopped wanting to do stuff together. You stopped—"

He shook his head. "No. It was before that."

And, very quietly, my brain said, "Remember? Remember the times way back in September, when Sal didn't show up to walk home together after school? Remember how he said he didn't have money to go out to lunch when you knew he did? Remember the morning you waited for him in the lobby until you were absolutely, positively going to be late, and then you rang his doorbell, and it turned out he'd gone to school without you?"

And then I remembered something else. I remembered running across Broadway holding my big *Mysteries of Science* poster, and seeing Sal on the other side, and yelling for him to wait up. And he had. He'd waited. And when I asked him why he wasn't at our regular spot after school, he'd just mumbled something and looked at his feet, and then we'd walked toward Amsterdam in total silence. Until Marcus hit him.

Sal had started home without me that day. And it wasn't the first time.

But here he was, today, looking right at me. And we still felt like *us*. "So when can we go back to normal?" I asked.

"That's the thing, Mira. It *wasn't* normal. I didn't have any other friends! Not real friends."

Neither did I! I wanted to say. And then I realized— that was his whole point. We'd only had each other. It had been that way forever.

He was still talking. "I mean, remember the second week of school, when you got sick? I spent that whole week alone. The whole week. Alone at lunch every day, alone after school . . . and don't take this the wrong way, but sometimes I want to hang out with boys." He yawned. "I'm on these pills," he said. "For my arm. They make me kind of sleepy."

"You could have just *told* me," I said. "You could have said all this stuff before. I thought we talked about everything."

"Not everything." He looked at me in a groggy way. "Anyway, I gave you hints. You never got them."

Mom and Louisa walked in. "I thought you might be getting tired," Louisa told Sal. "These painkillers!"

she said to Mom. "He takes one, talks his heart out for twenty minutes, and then falls asleep, like clockwork."

She gave me a tight hug as we were leaving and said, "I'm glad you two had a chance to talk." And I wondered if she'd saved the twenty minutes for me on purpose.

Things You Protect

Wheelie was running late. "I'm still working on the list," she said, pushing some candy across her desk at me. "Have a seat. I'll be done in two jigs."

That was fine with me. In the two days since the accident, I'd thought about your notes a thousand times and tried at least that many times to push away the memory of your body lying in the street. I wasn't sleeping much, and I was tired.

My first Bit-O-Honey was just softening in my mouth when two police officers walked into the office.

Wheelie looked up from her typewriter. "May I help you?"

"There a Marcus Heilbroner enrolled here?"

Her face stayed blank. "I believe there might be. But the principal isn't in right now, and—"

"That's okay. We just need a word with Marcus Heilbroner. Seems he likes to chase kids into the street, and we need to have a word with him about that. What room?"

She scratched her head. "I'm not—I'm not sure. I'll have to look him up."

That's when I got scared. Wheelie knew every kid in the school, and she knew what classrooms they were in without having to think about it. She was afraid, I realized. For Marcus.

I stared at the backs of the two officers and thought about the things Mom had told me about people who go to jail, about how some of them were never the same afterward. I couldn't let that happen to Marcus. He was barely regular to begin with. I thought of him shaking and crying on the curb after the accident, and how he'd tried to stop Sal from running in front of the truck, and how he'd been too clueless to realize Sal was running away from him in the first place.

"I need to use the phone," I said to Wheelie.

"This phone?" She put one heavy hand down on top of it. "I don't think so."

"Please!" I said.

"No, ma'am!" From behind her desk, she pulled out a plastic tub full of index cards and started to flip through them while the officers watched.

"Let's see," she said. "Hillerman, right? Any idea what grade he's in?"

They looked at each other. "Heilbroner," one of them said. "Don't you have an alphabetical list?"

"Of course!" she said. "But that's down here some-where. . . ." Her voice trailed off as she started to roll her chair toward the file cabinets that stood along the back wall.

I left the office casually, as if I just had to go to the bathroom, and then I sprinted around the corner and down the dead-end hallway. In my mind was a picture of the dentist's white wall phone.

The dentist was relaxing in his chair, looking very comfortable with a paper cup of coffee and the newspaper. "Hi, Miranda," he said, sitting up. "You have the patient list?"

"Can I use your phone?" I called to him. "It's an emergency!"

He looked surprised but said, "Sure, go ahead."

I called my mom at work.

"I need help," I said. "The police are at school and I think a kid is going to get arrested. A friend."

"But—all the lawyers are in court," she told me.

I started to cry. "Can you come, Mom? Right now?"

"Me?" she said. And then, "Yes. I'm coming."

By the time I hung up the phone, I had the dentist's full attention. "What's up?" he said.

"Marcus is in trouble," I said. "The police are here and they might arrest him and he didn't even do anything wrong! If my mom can get here I think she can help."

"Marcus is a good kid," he said firmly. "A good kid through and through." He calmly folded his newspaper and took a pen from his pocket. "So, Miranda, are you my runner this morning?"

I raced up the four flights to Marcus's classroom, the dentist's scrawled note in one hand, and burst in, yelling, "I need Marcus!" and waving the piece of paper in Mr. Anderson's face.

"Calm down! What's wrong with you?" Mr. Anderson stared at me, and I tried to stand still. He examined my note. "All right, Marcus, go ahead."

Marcus nodded and started rearranging the pile of books on his desk.

"Leave your books," I called to him. "The dentist says he needs you right *now*."

Out in the hall I said, "You need to hide. The police are here and I think they want to arrest you!" I started running toward the stairs.

Marcus called quietly after me, "It would probably be better if we walked."

He was right. Five seconds later, we strolled right past the police officers on their way up to Mr. Anderson's classroom. They didn't even glance at us.

The dentist locked the door behind us. Then he looked at me. "Your mom is a lawyer?"

"Sort of."

"Okay. We'll just sit tight until she gets here."

The police didn't come to the dentist's office right away—it must have taken them a while to find it. Nobody seemed to be helping them much.

They knocked, and the dentist called out, "Sorry, I have my hands full here. It'll be a minute."

I was wondering what we would do when a minute was up. The dentist just sat there reading his paper. Marcus looked at his palms. "I wish I'd brought my book," he said, turning to me accusingly.

"You're welcome!" I said. "I'm trying to save you, here."

"Does either one of you have a sense of what this is all about?" the dentist asked.

Marcus and I exchanged looks.

"I tried to stop him," Marcus said.

"I know. He was afraid of you."

He pressed his hands to his chest. "Of me?"

"You punched him! Remember?"

"I know!" Marcus put his head down on his two fists. "Oh, God," he mumbled, "and now that man is dead. That old man. He was afraid of me too. Remember how he ran away from me? But I never did anything to him! I swear!" His voice cracked and his shoulders started shaking.

"It wasn't your fault," I said quickly. "He—" But I didn't know what to say. Because it *was* kind of his fault. Marcus didn't mean for any of it to happen, but if he hadn't run after Sal, and Sal hadn't run into the street, wouldn't you still be alive?

The dentist was staring at us. "On second thought, it might be better not to talk," he said, nodding at the door.

Time crawled. The police waited, knocked, waited again, talked into their walkie-talkies, knocked again, disappeared, came back, knocked again, and then started calling out things like: "He better be in there when this door opens, doc."

And the dentist called his own stuff through the door, about anesthesia and paste-drying time, and only having two hands. It didn't make a lot of sense.

Marcus stared at the floor, which I'd just noticed was tiled with tiny white hexagons like the ones in our bathroom at home. My brain sorted the hexagons into the usual shapes and flowers. It was weirdly comforting.

Then, very quietly, Marcus said something. "I have an older brother. Anthony."

I looked over at him.

"I want you to know why I hit your friend that day—"

"Sal! His name is *Sal*. God, why don't you ever remember anyone's *name*?"

The dentist shushed us.

Marcus made his voice even lower. "The day before I hit Sal, my brother Anthony said something about another kid's girl. I think he meant it as a joke. But this guy got Anthony up against this car, and he was hitting him and hitting him. . . ."

I remembered. Sal and I had crossed the street to avoid that fight. Marcus's brother was the kid who had been trying to get off the hood of the car. Who kept getting knocked down. "I think I saw that," I said. "Was your brother wearing a hat?"

Marcus nodded. "Yeah. He always wears that hat."

"What did you do?"

"Nothing. I was leaning in our doorway, watching. Afterward, Anthony said to me, 'Did you even *think* about standing up? About helping me?' He said I was like no brother at all."

"Those kids are bigger than you," I said.

Marcus shook his head. "It wasn't that. I wasn't afraid. I just didn't see myself as . . . part of what was happening. Sometimes I'm thinking about stuff and I walk right past my own building. Those guys don't see me as one of them. Because I'm not one of them.

"Anthony told me, 'One day, you're gonna have to hit someone. And get hit yourself. Then you'll see. Maybe. Maybe you'll understand life a little better.' And I wanted to understand life better. To understand *people* better. So the next day, I walked over and hit Sal. And then I stood there like an idiot and waited for him to hit me back. But he just bent over and cried, and I didn't know what to do, so I walked away. And Anthony yelled: 'What the hell was that?' And later, at home, he said, 'What are you hitting short kids for? Don't you know nothing?' He said I was hopeless."

I was trying to think of what to say when Marcus suddenly looked at me with his eyes all wide. "Hey! You were the one holding the poster."

My mouth fell open. "You just figured that out?"

He nodded. "Interesting poster," he said. "I've always wondered about yawns. I read an article once—"

Then there was a fast clicking sound that I knew: Mom's heels on a hard floor. I shushed Marcus and pressed my ear to the closed door even though the dentist kept waving me back.

"I'm from the law firm of Able and Stone," I heard her say. "Can I help you gentlemen?"

"Only if you have the key to this door," one of the police officers growled.

She kept going. "I've spoken with the school secretary. I understand you want to talk to a student by the name of Marcus Heilbroner."

"Yeah."

"Mr. Heilbroner, as you certainly know, is a minor. We can use the principal's office for a few minutes so that you can brief me about whatever allegations have been made. But of course you can't speak with Mr. Heilbroner himself until his parents have been notified. Would you follow me, please?"

One of the police officers swore, but the other one said, "Might as well. We aren't getting anything done standing in this hallway." And they all walked away.

"Thank God." The dentist let out a long breath. Marcus stood up, but the dentist said, "Sit down. She hasn't gotten rid of them yet."

Another fifteen minutes went by while Marcus looked at the floor, the dentist paced, and I stared out the window. Finally we heard Mom coming back down the hall.

"They're gone," she called, "open up." I yanked the door open, and there she was with her hair pulled back, wearing a gray wool skirt and a matching blazer.

I flew at her and grabbed her around her tiny middle, almost knocking her down.

I felt her hand on my head. "Let's try to figure this mess out. Who wants to talk first?"

Things You Line Up

It turned out that Belle was the one who had reported Marcus to the police. She'd seen the whole thing from her store window and thought that Marcus had chased Sal into the street on purpose. So Mom was able to get things sorted out. She got a statement from Sal, who had to sign it with his left hand because of his cast, and one from me, and one from Belle, and by the following week, the police had dropped the whole thing and Mom had dressed like a grown-up for three days in a row.

"You know, you look darn good in a suit," Richard told her.

I figured she would give him some kind of lecture, but Mom took his hand and said, "Thanks. That means a lot coming from you, Mr. Perfect." She looked happy, and it seemed so obvious at that moment that they should get married. But she still hadn't even given him a key.

And then Mom hung up her suit, and I put all your notes in the box under my bed and didn't look at them anymore. Annemarie had her birthday party with two cakes, an awful one that Julia and I made for her and a really good one her dad made.

Time passed. Annemarie and Julia helped me install my playground on Main Street, and Julia's UFO finally got approved by Jay Stringer. I became Alice Evans's regular bathroom partner—we worked out a secret signal so that she wouldn't have to do the Mexican hat dance anymore. Marcus and I waved hello to each other, and we sometimes talked a little, except when he didn't notice I was there, which was about half the time. In early March, we started rehearsing songs for graduation. I kissed Colin a few more times, and I suspected that Jay Stringer was working up the nerve to kiss Annemarie. I don't think anyone dared to kiss Julia.

Sal's cast came off and he started playing basketball in the alley again. A couple of times I waved at him from the window, and once he yelled up to say hi and ask if I wanted to check out his three-point shot, which he lined up for about five minutes and then missed. I clapped anyway, and he took a bow.

I tried to forget about the laughing man. I mean, I tried to forget about you. But it didn't work. There was something left over: the letter I was supposed to write.

This is the story I need you to tell.

Please deliver your letter by hand. You know where to find me.

Trying to forget really doesn't work. In fact, it's pretty much the same as remembering. But I tried to forget anyway, and to ignore the fact that I was remembering you all the time.

And then, three weeks ago, Mom's postcard came from *The $20,000 Pyramid.*

April 27th: Studio TV-15. The last proof.

That's when I officially gave up the forgetting and started doing all this thinking. I have the story laid out in my mind now, as straight as it's ever going to be.

And now I'm wondering if I should just write the letter, even though you're dead and most likely buried on that island. I wonder if I should write it anyway, if maybe then I'll be able to stop thinking about you, once and for all.

The $20,000 Pyramid

Richard, Louisa, and Sal are coming with us to ABC Studio TV-15 on West Fifty-eighth Street to see Mom try to win twenty thousand dollars.

"Miranda, can you get me my sweater with the little buttons?" Mom asks. She's nervous, and her voice sounds too high. "If it's chilly in there I won't be able to concentrate."

"Mom, it's seventy degrees out," I say.

"Exactly. They might have the air-conditioning on. I'm always too cold in air-conditioning."

I get the sweater and check myself out again in Mom's closet mirror. I have on new jeans and a long-sleeved shirt with flowers embroidered on the sleeves that I borrowed from Julia. Richard has even polished my shoes for me with his special shoe brush. I try to fluff my hair, but my brain says, "What in the world are you fluffing your hair for? You know your hair doesn't fluff!" and I stop.

Richard buzzes from the lobby. Mom rushes to the intercom and yells, "We'll be right down! And happy birthday!" We walk downstairs and stop at Sal and

Louisa's door, which flies open as if they've been standing right inside waiting for us.

"The big day!" Louisa says. "Big day, big day, big day!" She seems even more nervous than Mom.

I look at Sal, and he shrugs and says, "She's been like this all morning."

We are very quiet on the subway.

There are people in red blazers by the studio doors.

"Contestants to the left," one of them says. "Audience to the right." And suddenly I realize it's time to say goodbye to Mom. She's standing there looking terrified and holding on to her bag with her sweater and her extra clothes and her barrettes. I go over and hug her while Richard gives her a kiss and Louisa says "We love you" and Sal looks at the floor and says good luck.

"You're going to win," I say. "I know it."

"Don't get your hopes up," Mom says, and then we watch her disappear behind a door.

We walk into the studio, which is like a theater with all the $20,000 *Pyramid* stuff up on the stage: Dick Clark's podium is there, and the word screens that swivel back and forth during the speed round, and two empty chairs facing each other in the Winner's Circle. Everything looks artificial and kind of gloomy in the dim light. I'm thinking that one good shove could probably knock the whole thing over.

There are a lot of people in the theater already, and we get seats about halfway back. They are red velvety seats, the kind you have to fold down before you sit on them.

A guy with headphones comes out and talks to the audience about when to clap and when to be quiet. He points to these metal boxes attached to the ceiling that light up like exit signs, only they say *Applause* instead of *Exit*. He explains that the signs will blink on and off to help us remember when to clap and when to stop. We have to practice with him: Clap, stop. Clap, clap, stop. It's a little silly, but Louisa and Richard are taking it very seriously. Sal and I laugh and dare each other to clap at the wrong time.

The stage lights come on, and suddenly the whole set is glowing like July at the beach. *Much* more cheerful. Richard takes my hand. Dick Clark comes out and says hi to the audience and Louisa starts talking about how she has always liked Dick Clark, how he has always seemed like one of the nicest people on television, and how now that she's seen him, she thinks she likes him even more. Isn't it amazing, she asks, how he never seems to age? He looks just the same today as he did back in 1956. She says she might ask him for some autographs after the show for the old people at her nursing home, because she's sure they would get a big kick out of that. Louisa is talking even faster than Mrs. Bindocker at the monthly tenant meeting. And then suddenly she is quiet. I look at her and see that she's biting her lips.

Everything starts to happen very fast. There is music. Dick Clark makes a funny face like he's afraid he might be late, and he hops over to his podium. The celebrities take the stage. I've never heard of either one of them. The next thing I know, Mom is coming out with her hair clamped back in barrettes, looking smaller than ever.

But she's wonderful. The speed round is a thing of beauty. Mom gets seven words out of seven every time, and wins the cash bonus. Her celebrity is not as dumb as a bag of hair. In fact, her celebrity is not remotely dumb.

The other contestant is good, but his celebrity speaks too slowly and says the word *bat* while giving clues for the word *batter*, an amateur's mistake. They lose that point and a couple of others. Before I know it, Dick Clark is leading Mom over to the Winner's Circle.

"This is it," I hear Richard whisper to himself. "Ten thousand dollars."

"Ten thousand dollars," my brain says. "Ten thousand dollars."

Mom's celebrity looks determined. Mom looks scared. Dick Clark is smiling. He's the only one who looks relaxed. He's chatting with Mom for a minute, and I know Mom is trying to focus, to lift a corner of her veil so that she'll be able to see the big things. So she can see the thread.

Dick Clark is still talking, and I realize: we never practiced the chatting. I am suddenly afraid. I am hearing the ocean. How can Mom lift her veil and see the magic thread with Dick Clark talking to her about her stupid job? I focus on Mom and try to help her concentrate. Louisa is getting nervous again, and she starts whispering about Dick Clark, "He doesn't age, I tell you. Dick Clark simply does not age. It's amazing." I'm chanting to myself, "Magic thread, magic thread," and I'm staring at Mom so hard that my eyes are almost aching.

Finally, Dick Clark is done chatting. "Here is your first subject," he says. "Go."

Then the strangest thing happens.

Magic Thread

Mom is jumping up and down, and I hear the sound of hundreds of people cheering and clapping, lifting me like a wave and carrying me. I am out of my seat, I am floating down the aisle, people are patting me on the back or reaching out to squeeze my arm, and then the stage is in front of me, I am going up some steps, and then light is everywhere, too bright, and it's hot.

Mom is still leaping around. She's hugging her celebrity, she's hugging Dick Clark. One of her barrettes is down by the side of her face, hanging on for dear life and banging against her cheek. She hugs me, and my head is pulled up and down as she jumps, so that I am forced to jump with her.

I feel happy. I smile and grab Mom's hands and jump up and down with her. I let go of her and raise my arms over my head and feel the audience roar louder.

I am not thinking of the wall-to-wall carpet, or the camera, or the trip to China.

I am jumping up and down because at the very moment Dick Clark said the word "Go," it was like an invisible hand reached out and snatched away my veil. And for almost a minute, I understood everything. When that veil isn't hanging down right in front of a person's face, a minute is long enough to realize a lot of things.

I realized that when you took our key from the fire hose, when you left me the notes, when you stole Richard's shoes and Jimmy's Fred Flintstone bank, you had already read my letter. You had read it many times, even though I have not yet written it.

That's how you knew where the key was, even before you asked. That's how you knew everything. I will tell you, in my letter. The letter you asked me to write.

"But that's impossible!" my brain squawked. "You're saying the laughing man read a letter that you haven't even *written* yet! It makes no sense!"

Common sense is just a name for the way we're used to thinking.

Time travel is possible.

You came to save Sal. And finally—finally!—I understood.

Dick Clark never ages. I thought of what Marcus had said about going to the movies in my time machine, that if I didn't leave until I was sixty-two, the ticket guy wouldn't recognize me.

I might not even recognize myself.

Maybe Dick Clark never ages. But the rest of us will. I will. Sal will, thanks to you. And Marcus will, too.

Please deliver your letter by hand, your note said. *You know where to find me.*

I thought of the beat-up metal door next to the garage, and I thought, "Yes, I do." Because you are still here after all, to read my letter. Marcus is here. And when he reads the letter, he'll realize that he has seen himself arrive, before he left. That's what my letter is for.

And then, in who-knows-what year—the year of the burn scale, the year of the dome—Marcus will come back. *You* will come back. You will come back with a mouth full of paper. You won't be yourself when you reach me but you will get the job done. You will save Sal. You already have.

Marcus is the magic thread. You are the laughing man. You are Marcus. Marcus is the laughing man. Or he will be, when he's old.

"None of it makes sense!" my brain yelled.

"But all of it is true," I answered.

Like I said, it lasted just under a minute. It lasted fifty-five seconds, to be precise. Which is how long it took Mom to guess six categories and win ten thousand dollars.

And then Mom and I are on the stage together, jumping up and down until they make us get off.

Things That Open

We take the bus home because we think it'll be so much *fun* to take the bus home, knowing that we are rich now and can take a cab anytime we want. And it is fun. Sal and I don't talk much, but we lean into the turns the way we used to when we were little and actually believed that we could make the bus tip over.

After Mom won her ten thousand dollars, she played another speed round. But this time she had to be partners with the other celebrity.

"He wasn't as dumb as a bag of hair," Mom says on the bus, "but he wasn't the sharpest knife in the drawer either." They lost. But Mom gets to keep her ten thousand dollars, and her twenty-one-hundred-dollar cash bonus. "Not bad for a day's work," she says, smiling at me. "Not bad at all."

When we get to the lobby, Louisa has to change into her uniform for work.

"Want to watch some TV?" Sal asks me.

I tell him I would love to. Another time.

Upstairs, Mom puts on a record, and she and

Richard dance for a while in the living room while I sit on the couch and grin, just watching them.

Then I go to my room, shut my door, and pull the box out from under my bed. Right on top of everything is a big envelope for Mom—Richard gave it to me a week ago for safekeeping. And underneath it is Richard's birthday present.

Mom is in the kitchen, making birthday tacos and a box cake. Every once in a while she yells, "Whoohoo! We're rich!"

I write on Mom's envelope with a marker: *I personally do not care about wall-to-wall carpeting. Louisa says carpets are full of dust mites anyway.*

I make an origami frog for Richard and put it on top of his box.

I make an origami frog for Mom and put it on top of her envelope.

I can't get enough of these origami frogs.

It's time for dinner. We eat the tacos. We sing. We cut the cake.

I give Mom her envelope. "What's this?" she says. "It's not *my* birthday!"

She admires her frog. She reads my note about the carpeting and the dust mites and gives me a funny look. She opens the envelope, which is full of applications for law school.

She looks at them. "But—I can't . . ." Then she sits back in her chair and says, "Wow."

This was our secret plan all along. Mine and Richard's.

I give Richard his present. He admires his frog and puts it on the table next to Mom's frog so that their little frog feet are touching. He opens the box. Inside are two keys, one for the lobby door and one for the apartment. I made a key ring for them—it's a sailor's knot, two strands, pulled tight. He knows how to untie it, of course, but I don't think he will.

Things That Blow Away

The next morning, I wake up early, cut myself a big piece of Richard's birthday cake for breakfast, and start writing the letter. I'm writing it in the journal with the clouds on the cover that Mom gave me for Christmas. I'm at the top of the second page when it dawns on me that this letter I'm writing is kind of a horrible burden. And I start feeling really sorry for Marcus.

It's not a letter that most people would want to get. I know it will be a big relief to know that he didn't accidentally cause the laughing man's death—your death—after all. That's a good thing. But at the same time, he'll understand that he saw his *own* death, which I have to think is a very hard thing. And he'll also realize that he's going to discover the secret of traveling through time, which is a thing so incredible that most people would consider it a miracle. Of course, he's the total hero of the story. But there isn't a happy ending for him.

I start at the very beginning, when you first showed up in the fall, and I'm thinking about everything you did—the spot on the corner where you stood, your kicking practice, the way you muttered to yourself. "Book, bag, pocket, shoe." There was a reason for all of it.

Except for one thing. I don't understand why you used to lie on the ground with your head under the mailbox. Why? It must have been annoying the way kids were always banging on it.

I raise my head slowly from the journal. Then I get dressed in a hurry, pulling a sweater on over my pajama top. I leave a note on the kitchen table, grab my keys, and slip out of the apartment before Mom and Richard wake up.

It's an almost-warm morning. No one is on the corner, which is good, because I probably look pretty strange lying faceup on the sidewalk and inching myself under the mailbox. It isn't as easy as I thought it would be.

The underside of a mailbox is really ugly—a bunch of paint-splattered metal joints and bolts. I see the square of paper right away. It's small, about the same size as the notes you left me, and it's wedged under a metal seam so that it stays flat against the bottom of the box. I realize that it's held there with a key—our old key, the one we hid in the fire hose. I adjust my head so that I'm looking straight up at the paper, the way you must have.

A woman's face stares down at me, drawn in pencil. She's old, like you were. Her white hair is pulled back behind her head, her dark eyes are looking to the side a little, and she has this playful smile. It's really kind of a beautiful drawing.

People can get old all different ways, I guess. Some people change a lot, like you. I could have stared at your face for a week and I never would have guessed that you were Marcus. You were so much thinner than he is, and the bones above your eyes stuck out. Maybe that was because of what you put yourself through— all the diamond-jumping. But the old woman's face in the drawing still holds some youth. It's the dark eyes, maybe, or the smile. It's hard to say exactly how we recognize other people. But I know without a shadow of a doubt that this woman is Julia.

Marcus and Julia. I think about how she whipped her diamond ring off and used it to explain the way she sees time, and the way Marcus stared at her afterward. Maybe he was thinking that he wasn't alone in the world after all. I get this rush of happiness, this flood of relief. Marcus won't be alone. He'll have a partner. He'll have Julia.

I'm wiggling out from under the mailbox—some guy with a big black dog is looking at me funny—and I suddenly remember what you said to me, practically on this exact spot, the afternoon I gave you my soggy cheese sandwich: *I'm an old man, and she's gone now. So don't worry, okay?*

I believe that you were ready. But I still think it's sad.

I leave the drawing there, wedged underneath the mailbox with our key. It doesn't seem right to take it. I figure it will be there for a long time, and then, someday, it'll just blow away.

Sal and Miranda,
Miranda and Sal

Sal and I don't wait for each other these days. Not purposely. But if we happen to be leaving school at the same time, if he isn't going to a friend's, or to basketball practice, and I'm not going to Annemarie's or Julia's—or Colin's—then Sal and I walk home together. And we are better this way, together because we want to be. He understood that before I did.

We walk up to Broadway, past Jimmy's. We walk to Amsterdam, past the garage, where the boys still say stuff to us and we ignore them. We walk past Marcus's door.

We pass Belle's. We cross the last street, to your old corner, where the mailbox is still scratched up with your words.

And when we are safely across, Sal always gives a little salute. And sometimes I look up, and shake my fist at the sky.

Parting Gifts

My letter is almost finished now. Very soon, I will bring it to Marcus, just like you asked.

There are things I could tell him, things I think I've figured out, like that those naked guys—the ones running down the street the days we had to eat lunch in the school cafeteria, and the one I saw flickering in and out before the accident—they were all you, learning how to get here. Practicing. You said you couldn't carry anything, and I guess that includes clothes. That's why you carried my notes in your mouth.

Or I could give Marcus some advice, like if he gets hungry while he's visiting, he'll find Annemarie's perfectly good lunch in the garbage can across from the schoolyard, where she threw it away every day for six weeks. But I'm pretty sure you figured that out for yourself.

Or I could tell him about Julia.

But I've decided I won't say much. I'll just hand him my letter and say, "Try not to land in the broccoli." He'll understand. He's a smart kid.

Acknowledgments

I had to be rescued several times while writing this book, and my profound gratitude goes to: my editor, Wendy Lamb, and associate editor Caroline Meckler, for their questions, advice, and trust; my agent, Faye Bender, for her insight and unflagging support; my wise and generous draft-readers, Deborah Stead, Karen Romano Young, Robert Warren, Jack O'Brien, Sean O'Brien, Samantha Kish-Levine, Michelle Knudsen, Alison James, and Daphne Grab, for their crucial aid and encouragement; the talented Colleen Fellingham and Barbara Perris, for their keen eyes and uncompromising copyediting standards; and art director Kate Gartner, for her delightful book design. Special thanks to Randi Kish, who opened her memory to me at a moment's notice, and to David Stead, who helped me understand my own story, once and for all, over breakfast.

Every writer stands on the shoulders of many other writers, and it isn't practical to thank all of them. However, I would like to express my special admiration for the astonishing imagination and hard work of Madeleine L'Engle, whose books captivated me when I was young (they still do), and made me want in on the secrets of the universe (ditto).

About the Author

REBECCA STEAD is the author of *First Light*. She grew up in New York City and still lives there, with her husband and their two sons.